Seeing him
was unexpected

Miranda asked, "Are you all right? You don't look...." Her voice trailed off helplessly.

He looked straight at her. "Miranda, come to bed with me."

Miranda closed her mouth and wondered wildly what to say. She licked her lips. "I couldn't do that, Mr. Barrett." Her words sounded inane and foolish to her, and she wished she'd just said no. "I think you're just trying to shock me," she went on. "I'm sure you didn't mean it—"

"But I did, Miranda," he interrupted as he moved forward.

She backed away but was stopped almost immediately by the door. Amusement gleamed in his intent dark eyes. He reached out to cup her shoulders. Miranda found her tongue again. "No," she whispered gently. "No, please!"

LINDSAY ARMSTRONG

enter my jungle

Harlequin Books

TORONTO • NEW YORK • LOS ANGELES • LONDON
AMSTERDAM • PARIS • SYDNEY • HAMBURG
STOCKHOLM • ATHENS • TOKYO • MILAN

Harlequin Presents first edition July 1983
ISBN 0-373-10607-6

Original hardcover edition published in 1982
by Mills & Boon Limited

CHAPTER ONE

THE stifled laughter in the court faded as the magistrate's gavel tapped authoritatively. He looked round sternly and then back to the girl in the dock.

'Would you mind repeating the sequence of events, madam,' he said. 'No, not right from the beginning. Let me see, I think we got waylaid,' he glanced round warningly, 'at the point where you were applying your lipstick. Please go on from there.'

Miranda Smith moved uncomfortably. She hadn't expected to enjoy this, but it had turned out far worse than her expectations. For one thing, she hadn't expected so many people to be present, hadn't at all expected to be the cynosure of so many eyes, and she found herself wishing fervently that a convenient hole would open up beneath her feet and swallow her.

The police prosecutor interrupted her thoughts.

'If I can jog your memory,' he murmured. 'You were on your way to an interview for a job. You were running late and hadn't had time to apply all your make-up. You got caught in a traffic jam and during the period of enforced inactivity you decided to apply your lipstick, using the rear-view mirror of your car. What happened then?' he asked with an infuriating blend of patience and patronage.

Miranda felt her cheeks burn. 'I didn't notice that the traffic in front of me had moved on,' she said stiffly. 'Then I realised everyone was hooting behind me and—I got a bit flustered, I suppose. I moved off and just as I came to the intersection the lights changed, seemed to absolutely race through amber,' she added, unable to keep a slightly indignant note from her voice,

5

'so that I was in the middle of the intersection on a red light, and this,' she swallowed, 'this great big black car had ploughed into me,' she finished uncertainly.

She blushed scarlet this time as she realised even the magistrate was having difficulty keeping a straight face now.

It took more than one tap of the gavel to restore order this time, and Miranda wished miserably she could die on the spot. She stared unseeingly at her hands and willed herself not to burst into tears.

But finally order was restored and when she dared to lift her eyes it was to look anywhere but at the magistrate and straight into the eyes of the only other man sitting at the prosecutor's table. He had taken no part in the proceedings as yet and had sat for most of the time with his head bent as he fiddled with a pencil.

Miranda had wondered who he was when she had first noticed him because there was something about him that had caught her eye. Perhaps it was his air of indifference or the way his well-tailored dark suit sat across his shoulders. Or the almost saturnine cleverness of his even features. But she hadn't had time to do more than wonder fleetingly—until now. And now she shivered inwardly as his sardonically amused, somehow remote and contemptuous gaze clashed with her own for an instant.

Then he looked down and the contact was cut as if with a knife, and Miranda jumped as the magistrate said sternly, 'Please pay attention, Miss Smith. I asked you if you were intending to claim that the traffic lights were malfunctioning?'

'The traffic lights were checked at the time, Your Honour,' the police prosecutor put in smoothly, 'and were found to be in perfect working order. Might I point out, if it hadn't been for the quick reflexes of the

Right Honourable the Minister's chauffeur, a much more serious accident could have occurred. Miss Smith should consider herself lucky that no one sustained any injury due to her—lapse in concentration, should we call it?' He sat down smiling gently as a ripple of mirth went round the courtroom.

Miranda bit her lip and found that her dreadful embarrassment had become tinged with a flicker of anger. It seemed that everyone was enjoying themselves at her expense and prepared to go on doing it. A certain stubborn light came to her green eyes that her family would have instantly recognised, and she tilted her chin slightly as she turned to the magistrate.

'Your Honour,' she said coolly, 'I never tried to deny that I was in the wrong. I'm certainly not doing it now. But I'd like to say one thing in my own defence. The prosecutor talks of the Minister's chauffeur and his reflexes, but where I learnt to drive I was taught that however much you might be in the right you should always proceed with due caution and not *shoot* off the minute the light turns green as he did . . .'

'And where *were* you taught to drive, Miss Smith?' the prosecutor interjected idly.

'Goondiwindi,' she said tautly, referring to the small outback Queensland town that was also her birthplace. 'What's wrong with that?' she added hotly, and for some reason looked at the prosecutor's companion, who was now sitting with his hands pushed into his pockets and a glint of outright laughter in his mocking dark eyes.

'Nothing!' the prosecutor said hastily. 'It merely crossed my mind to wonder how many traffic lights there are in Goondiwindi. Is it one or two?' he asked politely, and sat down with an incredibly smug look on his face.

But the crowning insult came as he said something inaudible to his companion, who shrugged and shook his head with quizzically raised eyebrows. Then they grinned at each other.

'Oh!' Miranda gasped. 'You think you're so clever, don't you? Well, I think you're insufferable!'

The commotion this caused was considerable and brought her a grave warning from the magistrate of being held in contempt of court. But she tossed her head defiantly, that flicker of anger now a steady, burning flame.

She said, jerking her head at the prosecutor, 'Is that what he's paid for? To make fun of me?'

The magistrate banged his gavel and pursed his lips as if struggling with his own mirth. But finally he said quite gently, 'How old are you, Miss Smith?'

'Twenty,' she said coldly.

'And how long had you been in Brisbane before this accident?'

'One week,' she said stonily.

'I see,' he said gravely. 'Your first visit? Ah.' He cleared his throat and looked at her steadily for what seemed a very long time.

She felt her colour rise and with clammy hands despite the chill of the air-conditioning, smoothed her skirt around her knees and unthinkingly fiddled nervously with the top button of her blouse.

Finally the magistrate spoke. 'Miss Smith, you've made a point that has a certain validity. It is everyone's duty to do all in their power to avoid an accident.' He looked down at the papers in front of him. 'One of the witnesses has stated that the official car was—I quote—pretty smart off the mark.'

He looked up and across at the prosecutor, who fidgeted suddenly.

'It has been claimed,' the magistrate went on

smoothly, 'that the reflexes of the other party involved prevented a more serious accident. A slower, steadier approach to driving in heavy traffic could perhaps be more beneficial than inspired reflexes,' he said sternly as the prosecutor made to rise.

'Quite,' he added as the prosecutor sank back. He turned to Miranda. 'Unfortunately, Miss Smith, this does not alter the fact that you entered the intersection on a red light. Therefore you are guilty of a breach of traffic regulations and a charge of dangerous driving, and it is my duty to determine a penalty, which I now do. You will lose points on your licence commensurate with the offence. You will also be fined. However,' he said dryly, 'I'm prepared to show some leniency in view of certain factors and apply the minimum fine I can by law.'

He named a figure and looked round quellingly at the surprised rustle.

Then he said quietly, 'You may go now, Miss Smith. But please bear this in mind. It is difficult enough to drive in heavy traffic without the added pressure of trying to apply your make-up at the same time. I caution you to give your driving your fullest attention in future.'

Miranda sat in a dim deserted corridor off the main passageway from the courtroom and tried to gather enough courage to leave the building. The walk through the courtroom had tried her composure sorely. And when she had realised how many laughing people were going to stream out behind her, she had ducked into this passage, found it a blind alley, so to speak, and sunk down on to a wooden bench.

Nobody had seen her as the chattering crowd had made for the main exit and gradually her hot cheeks had cooled and her hands had stopped shaking.

'But I can't hide here for ever,' she muttered to herself. 'Surely they must be all out by now?'

She stood up hesitantly and froze at the sound of approaching voices. The now deserted main corridor seemed to act like an amplifier, and it was with a start that she recognised one of the voices.

'. . . really thought the old bloke was past it,' the police prosecutor was saying. 'Minimum fine,' he mimicked in more deliberate tones. 'Who'd have thought it from a fresh country girl straight from the bush?' he added, reverting to his normal voice.

'I don't think it makes much difference,' a deeper voice answered. 'Most women seem to fall out of their cradles knowing just what a pair of legs and a straining button across the bosom can do.'

Miranda gasped incredulously and shrank back as the voices came closer.

'Unless he was feeling fatherly,' the prosecutor was saying with a chuckle.

'I doubt it,' his companion commented dryly, and Miranda moved sharply and clenched her fists as the two strolled into view and almost immediately out of it. For despite the brief glimpse she got, there was no mistaking the set of that dark suit moulded to the broad shoulders beneath it.

She crept forward trembling with rage so that she could peep around the corner, only to see that the two men had stopped a few yards away with their backs turned to her but close enough for her to hear the rest of their conversation quite clearly.

The prosecutor was saying, '. . . may have been a buxom bushie, but she had a streak of spirit too.'

Then *he* said, and Miranda cringed at the amusement in his voice, 'Yes. Perhaps someone should stick a label on her like—Keep me on the grass! Or—Beware!

Keep her hands on you and off your car!'

The prosecutor laughed delightedly, and Miranda leant her forehead on the wall and gritted her teeth as tears of humiliation ran down her cheeks.

But it wasn't quite over, she realised, as she heard the prosecutor say genially, 'Not quite your type eh? Got to admit she was stacked, though!'

She lifted her tear-streaked face to see the other man shrug offhandedly. 'Oh, I don't know,' he said with irony. 'If she handed herself to me on a platter, I guess I could put it down to experience. But I think you'd either have to be very young or very jaded to enjoy the attractions of our friend Miss . . . Miranda Smith for very long.'

He turned away and added casually over his shoulder, 'See you later.'

And Miranda watched him disappear through a doorway with suddenly dry, hate-filled eyes.

She found she was still quivering with rage and humiliation when she got home. She stood for a long time seeing her room with new eyes. She'd been so delighted with it three months ago, for although it was only part of a large, old-fashioned wooden boarding house, she had made it comfortable and attractive with touches of her own and it had its own bathroom, which for a stockman's only daughter with four lusty brothers was an unheard-of luxury.

But now, today, this room only seemed to laugh at her. Laugh at her along with the rest of the world, and she realised that all she wanted to do was pack her bags and head for home.

Home.

The thought brought her up short. What would it really achieve to go home? Wouldn't it only be acknowledging that they were right and she was wrong, although they never said it?

And the worst part, she thought miserably, is that they *won't* say anything either when I get back, my beloved family. They won't ever say I told you so, although they'll be thinking it quietly each in his own mind. Thinking, good! Now she's got that out of her system, she might settle down and marry Bill . . . Am I any more ready to do that than I was when I left? In three short months have I had a chance to find the answer to that strange restlessness I felt? That feeling of being trapped. I do love Bill in a way, but . . .

She sank down wearily into the only armchair the room boasted.

'But then there's question of money,' she acknowledged aloud with a heavy sigh. 'I knew it was going to be a battle. I didn't realise how hard it would be to get a decent job with my qualifications, or lack of them, rather.'

She grimaced as she thought of her bright dreams when she'd first arrived in Brisbane. Dreams of working at something interesting, saving some money and then exploring a bit of Australia at least before . . .

'Before I decided to tie myself to a corner of South Western Queensland where the sun never sets on talk of cattle, weather, horses.' She leant her head back against the chair and closed her eyes. 'And tie myself to Bill Hartley,' she whispered, and felt tears prick her eyelids as she thought of Bill.

She lowered her head into her hands and flinched at the tide of homesickness that flowed through her. I miss them all so much, she thought torturedly, and wrapped her arms around herself as if to still the pain. But to go home now?

She breathed deeply then and forced herself to study the alternatives. The only job she'd managed to get so far in these days of unemployment, even for more qualified people, was working three days a week in a take-away food shop. Not quite the stuff dreams are made of, she thought dispiritedly.

But for all its shortcomings it paid the rent, and she'd been using the money she'd saved before coming to Brisbane to pay for a night secretarial course upon which she had been pinning great hopes. Now—almost at a single stroke, she thought bitterly, this fine, for all it was the minimum, just about wipes out my savings and consequently my secretarial course.

'Minimum,' she murmured, and bit her lip as her thoughts fled back to the court room and what she had heard afterwards. She got up and crossed to the long mirror set in the wardrobe door and studied herself critically in old, uneven glass.

But all she could see was what she always saw—a fairly tall girl with luxurious, streaky fair hair and a good figure. Her clothes were quite ordinary, not expensive but not violently out of date, and not particularly countrified, she mused, and wondered wryly how one did look countrified, or rather like a fresh country wench?

'And buxom,' she muttered through her teeth as she stared at herself. 'If they really wanted to see a "buxom bushie" they should see Shirley Tate! Then they'd know the meaning of the word stacked. And my buttons do not strain—although I must admit Shirley's do often.'

She tried to smile, but it was such a weak effort she turned away from the mirror and blinked away a fresh set of tears.

He looked like the kind of man you could dream about, she thought. Well—yes, you have to admit it, Miranda, she acknowledged wryly.

She poured herself a glass of water and shivered suddenly as she recalled the mocking contempt in the man's eyes as they'd caught and held her own for that brief instant. And remembered how the well-tailored, conservative suit had only served to highlight the tall, beautiful body beneath, the way his thick dark hair had laid on his forehead and the clever asceticism of his face and eyes that had been so contradicted by his later words.

'So arrogant,' she murmured, and winced at the shaft of anger and pain that shot through her at the thought of his 'labels'.

Then she thrust out her chin and banged her glass down on the table. How dare he judge me like that! she thought fiercely. All of them for that matter. Anyone would think I'd come from the other side of the moon instead of only a few hundred miles away! Anyone would think I'd gone into that courtroom barefoot and sucking a stalk of hay. But I'll show them . . .

'It's just going to take a little longer, that's all, but I'll do it,' she vowed as she brushed away her angry tears with her hand.

CHAPTER TWO

MIRANDA consulted the piece of paper in her hand and stared up at the board in the foyer of the building she had just entered.

It was a very impressive marble foyer and when she found the floor she needed, a uniformed commissionaire ushered her into the lift.

She stepped out at the fourteenth floor and looked around. Barrett was the name she needed to find, and she found it almost immediately opposite the lift. She knocked on the solid teak door with its gold lettering and entered as bidden.

A middle-aged woman looked up from a large desk and removed her glasses. 'Can I help you?' she enquired in a well-modulated voice.

Miranda smiled. 'The employment agency sent me,' she said. 'About the position of cleaning lady?'

'Ah yes! Sit down, my dear.' She pulled a notepad towards her as she indicated a chair. 'Let's see, you'd be Miss Miranda Smith—is that correct?'

Miranda nodded.

'And I believe you've held this kind of position before?'

'Yes. I have a reference.' Miranda pulled a piece of paper from her purse and proffered it.

'I suppose it seems a bit strange to you to be here when the position advertised was for a private home,' the woman said conversationally as she put her glasses on and scanned the reference, 'but the fact of the matter is, I'm Mr Barrett's private secretary—he's a bachelor, you see, and I do all his hiring and firing for him. He doesn't really have the time either. And he has rather a lot of valuables in his home, so we have to check prospective staff rather thoroughly. I hope you don't mind?' She looked up with a disarming smile.

'No,' Miranda said quietly.

'By the way, I'm Mrs Marshall,' the older woman introduced herself. She looked back at the paper and a faint frown came to her forehead as if she was trying to recall something. Then she looked up and it was there in her eyes—a sort of speculation. Miranda tensed and wondered what it was that was bothering her.

But all Mrs Marshall said was, 'I see you come from Goondiwindi? How long have you been in Brisbane, my dear?'

'Nearly four months.'

Mrs Marshall pondered and for a fleeting instant Miranda thought her lips twitched faintly in amusement. Then she said, 'Would you like to join me in a cup of coffee? No, it's no trouble,' she added as Miranda moved and looked surprised. 'See, I have the pot here already. It's merely a matter of getting another cup.' She reached into a cupboard behind her and produced a cup and saucer.

'Now then,' she said when she'd poured the coffee, 'tell me about this previous job.'

'Well, my father is employed as head stockman on a large cattle station. Until I came to Brisbane I'd lived there all my life and when I left school I worked in the main homestead on the station. They had a lot of valuables too.' Miranda stopped abruptly and bit her lip. 'I wasn't being sarcastic. It's just that I do know how to care for silver and fine furniture and how to set a table and so on.'

'And how to cook,' Mrs Marshall murmured as she scanned the reference. 'In fact your former employer,

Mrs Wright, gives you a glowing reference.' She sat back and removed her glasses. 'You do realise this position will only be for say three mornings a week, Miranda, don't you? I mean, with these qualifications you could probably get a position as a live-in house-keeper. A more elevated position?'

'I don't really want that,' Miranda said hesitantly. 'I do have another job, you see, and I'd rather be more independent. Living with a family, however good they are, ties you down. But I do need to earn some more money. I'm attending night school, doing a secretarial course, and I'd like to finish it.' She grimaced faintly.

Mrs Marshall's keen gaze swept over her curiously. Then it changed to a look of warmth that Miranda found touching.

Mrs Marshall said, 'Mr Barrett can be a little . . . difficult sometimes. As I very well know,' she added with a glint of humour.

Miranda felt a strange tide of wariness creep over her. 'Is he . . . I mean, is he young or . . .?'

'Not young,' Mrs Marshall said briskly. 'And I don't mean difficult in that respect,' she added with a keen glance. 'But he can be moody and—prickly, if you know what I mean. Not that you'd be seeing a great deal of him. And he's prepared to pay rather hand-somely for someone who works well.'

'I see.'

'Good. The job's yours. When would you like to start?'

Miranda blinked. 'Any time,' she said dazedly. 'But what if he doesn't like me?'

'Well, he left it entirely up to me,' Mrs Marshall said on a faintly grim note. 'And my judgement's never let me down before. By the way, I should have mentioned this before. He gives the odd dinner party, generally at weekends, though. There could be work for you there if you wanted it. Could you cope with all three? Your other job, your night classes, etc.?'

'Well, I could try. I used to help Mrs Wright out like that.' Miranda looked at Mrs Marshall a little helplessly. She hadn't expected to get the job so easily.

But that good lady only nodded cheerfully and handed her a slip of paper. 'Here's the address. Why don't you go and see him first thing tomorrow morning? You can arrange a mutually suitable timetable. I'll let him know you're coming. I hope I see some more of you, my dear,' she added with a warm smile.

Miranda spent some time considering what she should wear the next day. An ageing, crabby bachelor raised unfortunate connotations in her mind. Like the magistrate, she thought tartly. Or rather the police prosecutor and his companion's reading of the magistrate. But then surely not all men think like that? she thought. And I only have *their* word for it.

However, the next morning when she stepped off the bus in a fashionable riverside area, she was dressed in one of her plainest dresses, a simple blue cotton that was demurely styled, and her naturally streaked fair hair was pinned back severely.

She took a bus, having decided that she couldn't afford to run a car any longer, besides being downright dangerous, and she'd sent her dilapidated vehicle home hoping that no one noticed the new bump on it.

The address she'd been given was that of an elegant, exclusive block of apartments set right on the river. She took the lift to the top floor and with a sudden outbreak of sweat on her brow pressed the bell of number forty-five.

The door opened almost immediately and she stood as if rooted to the plushly carpeted passage floor, as her mouth dropped open and she stared once again into the eyes of the last man she wanted to see.

It was hard to say, she realised afterwards, who was the more surprised, but there was no mistaking those dark eyes or the set of his shoulders, or the sudden frown of recognition that came to his eyes.

'I . . . I think I've made a mistake,' Miranda stammered, and backed away. 'I must have got the wrong number. It must be *thirty*-five . . .'

'Hang on!' he said peremptorily as she turned away hastily. '*Smith*?' Our friend Miss Smith? I don't believe it,' he added flatly.

'There's nothing to believe,' she mumbled. 'I just got the number wrong. Unless you're Mr Barrett? But you couldn't be,' she said on a rising note of panic. 'I'm sorry to have disturbed you.'

'But you haven't,' he said lazily, and reached out a hand to detain her. 'And I am.' He swung her round to face him.

'You can't be,' she burst out incredulously. 'Mrs Marshall said you were old!'

'Oh, did she?' he countered ironically. 'How old?'

'Well,' said Miranda with a tremor in her voice, 'she didn't say precisely, just that you weren't . . . young.'

'Dear Mrs Marshall,' he murmured, looking fleetingly amused. 'I'm thirty-three, to be more precise,' he added, 'and I am Nicholas Barrett and I don't know of any other. While you, I presume, are the Miss Smith I'm supposed to see this morning for the position of cleaning lady. Unless there are any other Miss Smiths lurking down the corridor?' he said idly but with a gleam of hateful laughter in his eyes.

Miranda gritted her teeth and flicked her wrist contemptuously out of his grasp. 'If I'd known it was you,' she said bitterly, 'nothing would have induced me to accept this job. Not for all the money in the world!' she added, and was so incensed to see that he was smiling openly now, she added furiously, 'So put that in your pipe and smoke it, Mr High and Mighty Barrett!'

She turned away decisively and tripped in her haste and as she steadied herself her purse slipped out of her fingers and scattered its contents on the floor.

She blushed bright scarlet and knelt down muttering a few choice words her brothers used occasionally but would have been horrified to hear her say. And snatched her hand away as her fingers encountered his lean strong ones.

'I can manage,' she said furiously. 'Why don't you go back to bed!' she added quite illogically, as he was fully clothed.

'I wasn't in bed,' he said smoothly, and wrested her purse from her to shovel a motley collection of objects into it. 'Tell me, do you take out extra accident insurance? Because I think it would be wise,' he said as he assisted her to her feet and handed her the purse with mock solemnity.

'Don't talk to me about accidents,' she muttered through her teeth, her eyes flashing green fire. 'Anyone would think I was the only person who'd ever had an accident in Brisbane!'

'You look very pretty when you're in a temper, Miss Smith,' he said with the corners of his well-cut lips twitching.

'Oh! Look, if . . . if . . .' she stammered in her anger, 'if I have to c-clean stables for the rest of my life, I'd rather do it than work for you!' She swallowed the hot tears that were threatening and then shut her eyes in exasperation as she realised that her heavy, silky hair was escaping the confines of the bobby pins she'd used so liberally. Then she tossed her head defiantly. 'Good day, Mr Barrett,' she said in as haughty a voice as she could muster. 'I hope I never see you again!'

'Wait . . . Miranda,' he said as if he'd had to dredge his mind for her Christian name.

'What for?' she said coldly as she tried unsucessfully to sidestep him. 'If you've got any more insults you can forget it.'

'And you can come inside,' he said forcefully, and manhandled her through the doorway despite her spirited resistance.

'How *dare* you!' she shot at him as he bundled her unceremoniously through to the lounge and sat her in a chair. 'Why are you doing this?' she demanded, and stood up as he moved away.

'I'd advise you to sit down,' he said coolly.

'And I'd advise you to go to hell!' she retorted, and stepped towards the door.

'Well, don't say I didn't try . . . Miranda,' he said lazily but with just that slight hesitation again that brought all her anger flooding back for some strange reason, to sweep away the sudden nervousness his actions had aroused. So that she turned towards him swiftly with every intention of slapping his face.

'Oh, come now,' he said with a mocking grin as he caught her raised arm deftly. 'What have I done to deserve this?' He clamped her arm to her side.

'Let me go,' she said tightly.

'That's all I was trying to do,' he murmured, his eyes glinting with laughter. 'And now all I'm trying to do is protect myself.'

'Oh!' she breathed, so angry now, she launched herself at him prepared to do anything to wipe that look of mocking, superior amusement from his face.

What followed was the second lesson of sheer humiliation Miranda learnt in the space of a few short weeks.

For despite her anger and the added strength it lent her, she ended up, most ignominiously, in his arms, or rather bent backwards over one of his arms which was round her waist like an iron bar, and with both her wrists pinioned in a savage grip behind her in his free hand.

She made one last desperate effort, but he didn't say a word, merely increased the pressure on her wrists so that her arms felt as if they were being torn from their sockets and her shoulders shot through with pain. And as a final insult, he let his gaze roam slowly downwards to her heaving breasts, then up again to her eyes.

They stared at each other for a long moment, Miranda with her mouth set mutinously while all she could read on his face was a kind of enigmatic detachment. Then the pain in her shoulders became too much and she closed her eyes briefly and sagged against him in a mute gesture of surrender.

He released her wrists immediately and with both hands about her waist sat her down in a corner of the settee and pulled her skirt decorously about her knees. Then he crossed to a silver tray which held an assortment of crystal decanters and splashed a tot of brandy into a glass.

'Drink it.' He offered her the glass, and after a slight hesitation she took it and sipped the liquid and felt the warmth of it calm her jangled nerves slightly. Then she put the unfinished glass down and stood up.

'I'll go now,' she said in a quiet, small voice.

'Sit down,' he said evenly, but there was no mistaking the warning in his voice.

Miranda sank back warily and looked at him uncertainly. He was standing with his back to a wide picture window that overlooked the river and she couldn't read his expression at all. She dropped her gaze miserably to her hands in her lap.

He moved at last and drew up a chair to sit down opposite her.

'Miranda,' he said abruptly, 'why don't you go home?'

The question shook her.

'Do you mean to Goondiwindi?' she asked, her voice husky with surprise.

'Yes. You have a family there, don't you? And perhaps a boy-friend? Maybe a few?'

'One,' she said tonelessly, and couldn't imagine why she was confiding in him. Or why she went on to say, 'At least there's someone there who wants to marry me. But I wasn't sure.' She shrugged. 'Sometimes you feel sort of . . . stifled up there. And after my mother died . . .' She stopped and bit her lip.

'Go on,' he encouraged. 'Tell me about your mother.'

'Well, she made me realise there was more to life than horses and cattle. She was a teacher, you see, and because I was the only girl in the family, we spent a lot of time together. We used to read together, anything we could lay our hands on, and talk—well, I think she tried to teach me all she knew. Not just the three Rs.' She stopped and looked up at him to see if he understood. He nodded and she went on with an effort. 'Then, after Ben was born, he's the youngest, we discovered she had a weak heart. Ben came some time after the rest of us and . . . and then she died, while I was doing my Junior Certificate. If only she hadn't tried to hide it from us,' she said her voice desolate.

'I'm sorry,' he said quietly.

'So,' Miranda went on, 'Ben was still quite little and I left school, although her dearest wish was for me to go on and do Senior. But,' she shrugged philosophically, 'there was no help for it. I stayed home for the next five years and worked part-time up at the homestead. It's not that I was miserable,' she said defiantly as she glanced up at him. 'I *love* them all. But Ted got married about six months ago, Ted's the eldest, and his wife came to live with us, and Ben's growing up so they don't need me as much.'

'And you started to get restless,' he said.

She plaited her fingers and sighed suddenly. 'Not only that, but everybody kept dropping sly hints that it was my turn next, you know how stupid people get, and how I'd be silly to let Bill Hartley slip through my fingers because not only does he have his own fencing business but Shirley Tate was always hanging round him, which seemed to me two very silly reasons for rushing into marriage,' she said, her eyes suddenly flashing fire as she thought of Shirley Tate. Then she added more calmly, 'Not that Bill himself was pushing me, but it all seemed to be getting on top of me, if you know what I mean? And,' she hesitated, 'well, I'm very fond of Bill, but I wanted to be sure. It was he who told me to come away. He was the only one who really understood.'

'He needs his head read,' Nicholas Barrett murmured with a wry grin.

Miranda stared at him. 'I don't know why I'm telling you this,' she said impatiently. 'I should have known you *wouldn't* understand! It's just . . .' She stopped.

'Just that you don't have anyone to talk to?' he queried perceptively after a moment.

'Not really.' She added defensively, 'I don't know anybody. It doesn't seem to be that easy to make friends in a big city. Not the kind of friends you can really confide in.'

'Isn't that all the more reason to go home?' he said after a moment. He sat forward. 'Miranda, I do understand what you were trying to say, but letting a girl like you loose in a city with not even a friend or a relative is just asking for trouble. I mean, you haven't exactly escaped it, have you?'

She took out her hanky and blew her nose. 'You make me sound like a stray dog that's bound to get run over,' she said bitterly.

'Which you did in effect,' he pointed out, with a faint grin. 'But . . .'

'All right, so I *did*,' she said wearily. 'But what does that mean? That I was nervous and flustered and keyed up because I was going for an interview for a job and the traffic was awful! I'm sure there are thousands of women drivers who feel as I did that day, only I was a bit more unlucky. What do you want to do, banish them all back to the farm? And I'll make friends. It just takes time,' she added with a shrug, and looked up to see a curiously intentness about him as he looked her over.

'With that luscious figure,' he said soberly at last, 'it might not take as long as you think. I'm afraid big cities can be rather like a jungle for someone . . . like yourself. Unless Bill Hartley has already . . .?' He looked at her with raised eyebrows.

'He has not!' she snapped angrily. 'No one has. And what kind of an idiot do you take me for? I'm not some innocent babe in the woods,' she added scornfully. 'I know what men are after and I've fought a fair few of them off, I can tell you. Boundary riders, jumped-up jackeroos who think you should be happy to keel over for them.' She stopped and looked straight at him. 'Do you *really* take me for such a ninny?'

Their glances locked and it was he who broke the sudden silence.

'It's bit different down here,' he said slowly. 'And that's what I was trying to point out. When you're lonely—well, put it this way, not all wolves come in wolf's clothing. There are slicker operators out there, and because you're lonely and feeling a bit adrift you sometimes become easier prey. You . . . lower your guard.'

Miranda moved restlessly because she couldn't help but recognise the wisdom of his words. But she said, 'Well, I'll just have to make sure I don't . . . lower my guard, as you so kindly phrased it, won't I? Because I'm staying! And what with night school and when I get a second job, I won't have time to feel lonely, anyway.' She met his gaze steadfastly.

'What are you studying at night school?' he asked seriously.

She told him. Then she paused before she said, 'It seemed to be the quickest way to achieve my independence. Once I can type and do shorthand, I get the feeling I could rule the world. By comparison to what I have to offer now, that is.' She grimaced wryly.

'I see.' He looked at her expressionlessly for a long time. Then he said, 'Forgive me for asking this, Miranda, but are you short of money?'

She considered how best to answer this or whether she really wanted to get into it with this man. Then she shrugged and said truthfully, 'Yes. What with having to pay board and other things.' Like the fine, she thought yet didn't mention it. 'But I'm not exactly destitute.' She smiled faintly and stood up. 'I think I ought to go now.'

Nicholas Barrett sat back. 'You're quite free to go,' he said evenly. 'But if you're determined to ignore my advice, the job is yours.'

She tensed at his words and searched his face, her eyes troubled. 'I couldn't,' she said gruffly at last. 'After the things I said. You—don't have to feel sorry for me.'

He stretched his long legs out impatiently. 'What I feel has nothing to do with the fact that you have the best qualifications for the job. Mrs Marshall would have made sure of that even though . . .' He stopped and waved a hand dismissively as he stood up himself.

'And yes, I do feel sorry for you,' he said wryly. 'But only because I don't usually go round hurting little girls.'

He put his hands on her shoulders and she stiffened immediately.

'Relax,' he murmured as his fingers massaged her

shoulders gently. 'No,' he added to her swift upward look, 'you don't have to look round for a heavy instrument. I have no designs on you, Miranda. I'm sorry I hurt you, but you did rather provoke me. Would it suit you to work tomorrow morning? I had in mind Monday, Thursday and Saturday mornings?'

Part of Miranda's mind seemed to have gone blank to anything other than the feel of his hands on her shoulders. The other part registered a vision of herself trudging around employment agencies and backwards and forwards to interviews, searching the positions vacant columns of the newspapers.

But still it was with a tinge of surprise that she heard herself say, 'Yes.'

He dropped his hands. 'Good,' he said briefly, and turned away. 'About eight o'clock would suit me,' he added over his shoulder as he picked up her purse and handed it to her. 'See you tomorrow, then,' he said with a casual grin as he ushered her into the vestibule.

'Yes,' she said again, and was about to go through the doorway when a sudden thought stopped her. She turned back.

'What were you doing there?' she asked. 'I mean, I know now you're a barrister, but I just wondered why you were there.'

'In court? I was instructed by the other party's solicitors to be there to protect their . . . interests.'

'Oh? I should have thought I was all the protection their interests needed,' she said ruefully. 'I'm sure everyone else thought so, judging by their amusement.'

He looked at her curiously with his eyes narrowed. Then he said, 'You know, you surprise me, Miranda.'

'Why?'

He raised his eyebrows quizzically. 'Well, you're not quite the ordinary run-of-the-mill . . .' He hesitated.

'Country bumpkin?' she supplied sweetly enough but with a sharp inner jab of irritation.

He laughed. 'You said it, I didn't.'

She shrugged and although for a moment she was tempted to fling his job back in his teeth she managed to bite her tongue and say, 'Oh, I don't have any pretensions about it. Well, I'll see you tomorrow.'

She turned and walked away as if she had not a care in the world, although in fact her thoughts on the subject of Nicholas Barrett, Q.C., which had undergone a subtle and unconscious revision during their talk, had now quite consciously reverted to their former opinion.

'Of all the cold, arrogant . . .' she muttered beneath her breath.

CHAPTER THREE

MIRANDA sang softly to herself as she wielded the iron on one of Nicholas Barrett's tailor-made shirts. Her voice had a curiously attractive huskiness and she sang because she was happy. A letter from home reposed in her pocket.

It was a long rambling, round-robin kind of letter, sometimes a bit hard to decipher. Principally written by her sister-in-law, there were notes in it from most of her brothers and her father. It seemed they were all well and happy but missing her. She smiled to herself as she recalled her brother Billy's missive. She had a particularly soft spot for her youngest-but-one brother, maybe because he was a bit of a rebel.

'Billy Smith!' Miranda could still hear her father's outraged tones. 'Just wait until I get my hands on you, Billy Smith!' It had become time-honoured saying at home.

But one bit of news in the letter had been particularly exciting. It seemed Miranda would be an aunt shortly.

She stopped ironing suddenly and thought, I know what I'll do to celebrate! I'll go out and buy myself a new dress this afternoon. It is pay day, after all, and I'm not quite so broke any more. I just wish . . . yes, Miranda? Wish what?

'That someone had mentioned Bill Hartley,' she said out loud with just a tinge of defiance. Then she gave herself an impatient shake as if determined to allow nothing to dim her happiness and reached for another shirt.

In the month she'd worked for Nicholas Barrett she

had quickly settled into a routine. Thursday was her laundry day, Tuesdays vacuuming and polishing and Saturdays she reserved for windows, walls and the kitchen.

And despite her very mixed feelings about her new employer, whom she rarely saw as Mrs Marshall had predicted, she couldn't help but take a certain amount of pride in keeping his beautiful apartment glowing.

Not particularly on his account, she often reminded herself tartly, but because it was so beautifully decorated and everything from the crystal and silver, the Persian rugs on the floor and the gold-framed paintings on the matt-beige walls to the solid woodwork of the silk and velvet upholstered furniture, seemed to come alive beneath her fingers. No one, she also often reminded herself, could fail to derive some pleasure, some feeling of reward from looking after this kind of stuff.

But two rooms of his apartment tapped slightly deeper emotions within her. The first was his study with its great oak desk and, particularly, the bookshelves that lined the walls. And when she dusted the books she often paused and, feeling guilty but unable to help herself, glanced through them. For there were not only legal tomes, she soon found, but a variety of literature from Shakespeare to Arthur Miller, and she often thought if someone locked her in there for a few days and threw away the key, she wouldn't really mind.

The other room was his bedroom. And the faint embarrassment she had felt whenever she entered the room, with its huge bed beneath its austerely fitted midnight blue spread and pure white carpet, had trebled during her second week when she had discovered a lipstick-smeared tissue in the en-suite bathroom and a hairpin on the floor. The implication of this was all too obvious because there was a second, guest bathroom in the apartment.

But she'd felt even worse a week later when she'd discovered a blonde chiffon negligee with swansdown about the wrists and neck, hanging behind the bathroom door. Worse, possibly, because she found she couldn't help herself speculating about this woman who shared his bed and what she was like. Very elegant, she decided. Or perhaps young and chic? But the worst part of these speculations was that they led her to think of her employer himself, to remember the feel of his fingers massaging her shoulders that day, the way he had looked in court, and these memories somehow left her feeling curiously shaken. It usually took a few moments of remembering some of the things he had said about her, and to her, to banish that feeling.

However, on this fine Thursday she wasn't plagued by any more serious thoughts than the new dress she planned to buy, and she gathered up all the shirts on their hangers and waltzed out of the laundry with one arm slightly round them as if she was dancing with them, pirouetted across the hallway singing as she went and stopped abruptly only inches from Nicholas Barrett, who wasn't supposed to be there but undoubtedly was.

He straightened up from where he'd been lounging against the doorway and looked at her with raised eyebrows.

'I didn't hear you come in,' Miranda said breathlessly, and lowered the shirts.

'That's obvious,' he drawled with a suspicion of a grin. 'I see you employ the whistle-while-you-work technique, only you sing.'

'There's nothing wrong with that, is there?' she said, flushing faintly and feeling unreasonably cross at being caught in another embarrassing situation. 'I used to sing in the church choir!'

'Oh, I'm not criticizing your voice,' he said easily. 'It just amuses me to think of you here working away and singing like a veritable canary. Yet another facet of Miranda Smith,' he added, and stood aside. 'I presume you were heading for the bedroom,' he said with the utmost gravity. 'After you, ma'am.'

He followed her into the bedroom and pulled off his tie as she hung up the shirts.

'Why . . .'

'Have you . . .'

They spoke simultaneously and Miranda turned from the built-in wardrobe and turned back almost immediately with wide eyes and hot cheeks, because he'd taken his shirt off as casually as he'd removed his tie.

'Go on,' he said to her back.

'I just wondered why you were here, that's all,' she said, her voice slightly muffled, and she then forced herself to turn round.

'I'm playing golf this afternoon. Which reminds me, do you remember that green T-shirt I wore a week or so ago? The one with the cream collar? I can't seem to find it. It's rather a lucky shirt too.' He grinned at her humorously.

'Er—have you looked in your top dresser drawer? I'm sure I put it there. I'll get it.' She moved past him with studiously averted eyes, hoping she wasn't still looking flushed. She found the shirt and took a deep breath. 'I rearranged your drawers. I hope you don't mind? They were a mess,' she said, trying to speak unconcernedly as she handed him the shirt, unable to avoid looking at him any longer. 'I hope you don't mind,' she went on less smoothly as her pulses raced because, as she'd always known they would be somehow, his shoulders were broad and smooth and tanned. 'I've finished, I'll go now,' she added hastily.

'Don't go yet, Miranda,' he said. 'I want to talk to you.'

'Well, I'll wait for you in the lounge,' she said as she beat a hasty retreat, and didn't see his quizzically raised eyebrows.

But once out of range and sitting primly in a wooden monk's chair with the river spread beneath her feet, or so it seemed, she chided herself for being so foolish and deliberately switched her mind to what he wanted to talk to her about.

'Maybe he wants to sack me?' she murmured to a large bulk-container ship tied up at the New Farm wharf.

'Nothing as drastic as that,' Nicholas Barrett's voice said almost in her ear, causing her to jump.

'How do you always manage to creep up on me?' she asked on a slightly indignant note as she turned to look up at him.

'Well, I think you ought to acquit me of that charge for my earlier arrival on the scene,' he said amusedly. 'You were so engrossed in your dancing and singing, I could have driven a tank in here and you wouldn't have noticed.'

'Do you always talk in legal terms?' she asked, because it was all she could think of to say as he sat down on the window seat and laughed at her.

'I suppose it's infectious,' he said gravely at last. 'After all, you often talk in bush vernacular, don't you?'

'I do not!' she said offendedly.

'No?' he queried lightly. 'What about that gem—jumped-up jackeroos?'

'Oh well,' she said with a small smile tugging at her lips, 'if you only knew some of them, you might describe them that way yourself.'

'But I do,' he said offhandedly. 'Having *been* one myself.'

'A jackeroo?' she said incredulously. 'I think you're having me on.'

'Not at all,' he countered. 'I was indeed a ... possibly jumped-up jackeroo on a station out from Barcaldine. It's a very fashionable pastime for the idle young of the rich while they decide which career to choose.'

'Don't I know it,' Miranda said cuttingly. 'And then when they decide, they flit through and leave ... well ...'

'Leave some surprising reminders of their sojourn? Is that what you were about to say?'

'Yes,' she said baldly.

'But not with you, I gather,' he queried seemingly idly.

'Not with me,' she agreed. 'But someone I knew rather well.'

'Who?'

'Shirley Tate,' she said without thinking, and then coloured.

'I'm never liable to meet this recurring Shirley Tate,' he said after a moment, 'so you might as well tell me.'

'She did ask for it,' she said painfully at last. 'But she was just so cut up I couldn't help feeling ... really feeling for her. And then when her family didn't know how to handle it, although in time I'm sure they'd have worked something out, she ... went bush and tried to do away with the baby. She nearly did away with herself too.'

'I hope ... she won't be branded with it for the rest of her life,' Nicholas said more seriously than she'd ever heard him talk.

Miranda shrugged. 'A lot of people surmised, but no one really knew apart from me and her family. And I took good care that they didn't ever know.'

'She came to you for help? I got the impression that you weren't . . . precisely soulmates.'

Miranda thought for a bit, then shrugged again. 'But we're both women and we'd known each other all our lives. I'd already suspected, you see. Only,' she paused then went on quietly, 'I don't think she really learnt from it. Do you know what I mean? If she doesn't snare Bill Hartley while I'm away, I get the feeling she'll fall like a big, soft ton of bricks for the very next bloke who chats her up.' She grimaced wryly. 'Just to prove she's not an outcast and . . . rejected.'

He glanced at her. 'That's not a peculiarly . . . bush failing, you know.'

She frowned. 'I didn't suppose it was,' she said tartly, and was about to lapse into an offended silence, but something about the way he looked got through to her. 'What do you mean?' she asked.

He looked out over New Farm. 'My sister suffers from the same malaise. She encountered a particularly painful rejection of herself not so long ago. Now she's trying to prove she's acceptable to all comers,' he said with a sudden grim twist to his lips.

'Oh dear,' Miranda said with her hand to her lips. 'But I can't believe *your* sister . . . You see, Shirley isn't—well, she isn't very bright, if you know what I mean. She just works on—instinct, I sometimes think. I can't believe your sister is . . .'

'A ninny?' he supplied, and moved restlessly. 'Actually I couldn't think of a more apt description. Clever enough in her own way, but all the same, over this, about as dim as Shirley Tate.'

'What does she do?' Miranda asked curiously.

'Do you mean when she's not living the high life, spending a fortune on clothes or redecorating her place? Nothing much. She was a journalist. Quite promising too,' he said coldly, 'until she allowed one worthless man to destroy her.'

Miranda shivered at something in his voice. 'Maybe she really loved him?' she offered tentatively.

'Oh, come on,' he said scornfully, and stood up impatiently.

'Don't you believe in love?' she asked after a moment as she eyed his tall, taut figure.

'To be quite honest, no, I don't think I do,' he said flatly. 'But if it does exist, it's being shockingly abused—I see examples of it every day. And if it's love that's brought about the destruction of my sister Sarah—well . . .'

He didn't finish but shrugged and turned away from the window to stare across the room with narrowed eyes and a set mouth and such a look of implacability that Miranda swallowed and couldn't help thinking how sorry she would feel for any woman who fell hopelessly in love with *him*.

'You'd know you were alive then,' she muttered beneath her breath, and jumped as he looked down at her at just that moment and raised his eyebrows enquiringly.

'Oh,' she said hastily. 'It doesn't matter. I was just wondering if you're the right person to try to help her.' She bit her lip. 'I mean, it's very hard to help someone you're so close to, isn't it? That's what I meant,' she added, and coloured as he looked amused.

Then Nicholas shrugged again and touched her hot face lightly. 'You're probably right on both counts. What you really meant and what you said you meant. Tell me, does this habit of yours of calling a spade a bloody spade get you into much trouble?' he asked quizzically.

'Now you're teasing me,' she said gruffly, still strangely aware of the feel of his fingers on her cheek although he had removed his hand and shoved it into his pocket. Miranda resisted an urge to touch her cheek with her own fingers. 'I didn't seem to have the problem until I came to Brisbane,' she managed to say with a wry grin, but she was thinking, why does he have this effect on me? It's not as if I haven't seen countless men without their shirts or been patted and hugged like a kid sister. What is it about him that makes me . . . feel like this? She looked up at him fleetingly and then downwards, and trembled inwardly as a tiny ripple of—was it fear? went through her.

'What are you thinking, Miranda?'

His amused words brought her out of her thoughts smartly and she said with an effort, 'I was just wondering what you wanted to talk to me about.'

He didn't answer immediately but looked more amused than ever briefly. Then he said, 'I'm giving a dinner party on Saturday evening. Do you work at your other job on Saturdays?'

She shook her head. 'Mondays, Wednesdays and Sunday from two until eight.' She looked up at him expectantly.

'Well, if you're interested in doing it for me, and Mrs Marshall seems to think you're quite capable of it, would you care to take on this dinner party?'

'You mean do it all?'

'Uh-huh. But what with shopping for it and cooking it, it might take you the whole day and most of the evening. How does that sound? Of course you could relax here too. I'd be out of your way.'

'How many people, and what kind of a menu did you have in mind?'

'Eight people in all, and I'm not fussy about the menu. Except to say I think three courses would be adequate and perhaps simple dishes that are really well cooked and served might be an idea.'

Miranda bit the tip of her finger and then smiled suddenly. 'I could do it. I did it for Mrs Wright. I could even pretend I was the Duchess of Duke Street—unless you wanted me to look like a maid?'

He stared down at her and she moved uncomfortably at the curiously intent yet enigmatic look in his dark eyes.

'I was only joking . . .'

'I wasn't laughing,' he said gently at last. 'And no, I don't want you to look like a maid. So I'll leave it all up to you, shall I? I've put some extra money in your pay packet to take care of the marketing. I'll see you some time on Saturday afternoon.'

Miranda delayed buying her dress until the next afternoon because Friday was her only free day and she now had a definite purpose in mind for the dress.

But she thought about it with happy anticipation until for some strange reason it made her thoughts jump to that day in court and what her employer had said—particularly about straining buttons.

It's strange, she mused to herself, in my heart I know that what they said about me was only part of this invisible sort of war that goes on between men and women. If some men think they've been outdone by a woman, well, they hit back with the best weapon they have. And that's to put you in your place and let you think you only have one use in life. Only in my case they had another weapon to use. So they made me out to be a seductive milkmaid fresh from the dairy.

But while I know this, her thoughts wandered on, why is it that that scar hasn't ever quite healed? Almost as if I'm having a hard time convincing myself of it.

'If it had only been the prosecutor,' she murmured aloud, 'I might not have minded so much. I could have hated him quite happily for being the epitome of male

chauvinism—or something like that. But because it was
...' Her words trailed off, but not her thoughts.
Perhaps I wouldn't have felt so bad if *he* too hadn't
sought to demolish me verbally like that. But really,
she thought then, what difference does it make? Why
don't you just forget it?

Nevertheless, as she planned her menu that night
and thought about the new dress, her thoughts were
tinged with a certain amount of defiance, a sort of 'I'll
show you' attitude which she recognised but couldn't
altogether suppress.

She had decided on roast pork for the main course
which was simple enough and she knew exactly how to
get the crackling perfectly crisp and the meat melt-in-
the-mouth cooked. And for the first course she'd
thought of cold vichyssoise which had been one of Mrs
Wright's favourite soups and seemed to suit the warm,
muggy weather.

For dessert, she had been torn between a cheesecake,
perhaps, or a pavlova, but in view of the fact that she
had a certain magic in her hands, or so her former
employer had reckoned, when it came to producing
the lightest, biggest pavlovas, she decided to stay with
her strength and planned to fill it with very cold fresh
fruit salad and cream, and garnish it with Kiwi fruit.
If she could find any.

'But first things first,' she told herself next morning
as she walked down Queen Street in the city just as the
shops were opening. 'I have to find a dress that doesn't
break the bank!'

She recognised *the* dress the minute she set eyes on
it. Superbly simple, beautifully cut, nothing that would
look as if she wished she was going to the party herself,
but all the same with a kind of elegance.

The saleswoman confirmed it. 'It's perfect for you,
my dear,' she said. 'It's the kind of dress you won't

ever feel underdressed or overdressed in. And you have
such a nice even tan that sets it off really well. I suppose you spent a lot of time down the coast?'

'Down the coast', Miranda had soon discovered,
meant one thing in Brisbane. The Gold Coast, which
was only about a forty-five-minute drive away. She
didn't enlighten the saleslady that the closest she ever
came to anything approaching those conditions were
the Centennial Baths at Spring Hill, a short walk from
her lodgings and in beautiful, uncluttered sur-
roundings with a golf course to look over so that you
could almost forget you were within minutes of the
heart of a city.

She looked at the price tag and then at herself in the
mirror in the cream dress with its fitted bodice and
slightly A-line skirt. She fingered the plain round
neckline and slightly cutaway shoulders. She felt the
fine, lined crepe and noted the way it was cut about
the bust, shapely but not unduly emphasising, and how
trim her waist looked.

'It's dear,' she said.

'A good cut and good fabric is never cheap, but you
get your money's worth in the long run. It's a perfect
basic dress that you could make into several different
outfits with perhaps a blazer or a silk scarf, necklets
and brooches which are very fashionable again, a different coloured belt . . .'

'I'll take it.'

'You should wear something green with it. A touch
of green would be perfect for your eyes,' the salewoman
added, and Miranda thought of her mother's necklace
which was perhaps her most treasured possession.

Miranda studied her reflection, but particularly her
hair. 'Should I get it cut?' she asked involuntarily.

'No,' the saleswoman said judiciously. 'It's beautiful.
Just shaped, perhaps.'

'Well, I will.'

When she got home she was tired but exhilarated. She hung up her dress carefully and put away her new shoes. Then she stood in front of her mirror and assessed her new haircut. She'd always cut her own hair, as had her mother, and the natural waviness had hidden the deficiency of her cutting technique. But she had watched the hairdresser very carefully as strand upon strand of streaked fairness had met the floor. She still had the length, in fact there wasn't a great deal of difference except that when she ran her fingers through it, it subsided beautifully. She swung her head and the same thing happened. She laughed and marvelled at the difference she hadn't perceived at first. She now had a head of much more manageable yet so natural-looking hair.

Saturday dawned bright and clear and the butterflies in her stomach increased as she rose early and packed a small bag with her new clothes, fresh underwear and a pinafore.

She shopped successfully for her ingredients, keeping careful note of what she spent, and then she let herself into the quiet apartment and set to work eagerly.

She made the vichyssoise first and then the pavlova and while it was drying out, chopped up the fruit salad, added a dash of cooking sherry to it and set it in the refrigerator. Then she did some cleaning and polishing and sorted out the table linen, and noticed for the first time a note from Nicholas Barrett. 'Should be back by six,' it said. 'Guests arriving at seven, expect to eat at eight.'

Miranda sorted out her own timetable accordingly and by two-thirty had nothing left to do. The apple sauce was made, the vegetables prepared, the flowers she'd bought arranged, the apartment gleaming and the roast ready to pop into the oven.

'Let's see,' she murmured, 'there's only the table to be laid and the nuts and olives, etc., to be put out, and the later I leave that the better. And after all, he did say I could relax here if I wanted to.'

She marched into the study with a small smile and curled up in the big chair behind the desk with *Wuthering Heights*. She'd read the book with her mother years ago but had found it hard to follow then and her mother had said indulgently to try again in a few years. Well, she'd never got round to it, but here was an opportunity.

But four o'clock came round surprisingly quickly and she reluctantly dragged herself back from the Yorkshire moors and the Earnshaws and stretched lazily. Then she jumped up to put the roast on and decided to have a shower and get dressed while she still had the place to herself.

'It's very quiet round here,' she said to the empty guest bedroom, conscious of the echoing silence, and switched on the bedside radio so she could hear it in the shower. But as she twiddled the knob all she could hear were either race broadcasts, advertisements or cricket commentaries.

She switched it off and stood poised for a moment with her chin raised. 'After all, he won't be back until six, will he?' she said aloud, and with a pulse of excitement ran into the lounge room to the magnificent stereo deck that was concealed in a mahogany wall cabinet.

She studied it carefully and thought that the basic mechanics of it didn't look too different from the one at home. But she hesitated, wondering if she was committing an awful sin, and flipped idly through the records. And once she did that, she was lost.

Miranda came from a basically musical family. All her brothers strummed guitars and had been through agonising periods as budding drummers. Her mother's piano had seen five children labour over its yellowing keys, although only Miranda had achieved any kind of proficiency, and even that was limited to Strauss waltzes, Marche Militaire and Für Elise. For a while it had been like a blight on her life that she wasn't going to be another Eileen Joyce, but it had been compensated for by the fact that she could always listen to music, especially after her father had bought the record player for her mother and together they'd started a collection of records.

But the records she flipped over now almost took her breath away. Mozart, Beethoven, Rachmaninov, Grieg . . . they were all there, her favourites plus many more. Also Billy Joel, Elton John, Don Maclean, but while she liked them too, in the right mood, her first love was the classical stuff.

She stopped flipping and closed her eyes. 'Will I? Yes, I will. I can't resist it, not the *Eine Kleine Nachtmusik*.' She opened her eyes and eased the record out of its sleeve. There was a picture of a marble bust of Mozart on the cover, and she smiled faintly as she very carefully put the record on the turntable because it was a particularly haughty-looking bust of the composer. Then she held her breath as she moved a button sideways, but the record began to rotate obediently and the arm lifted smoothly and dropped on to the record precisely and unhurriedly. Then the lovely music began to flow, and throwing caution to the winds, Miranda drifted into the kitchen as if she was moving on a tide of it and poured herself a small glass of cooking sherry. She took the sherry into the bathroom with her, her mind totally absorbed with the music, and took her clothes off and stepped into the shower. She had left the door open so she could still hear it, unaware, as the music swelled that the magnificent speakers were far more powerful than the ones at home, and that without the benefit of being in the shower with the water gushing, the whole apartment was alive and throbbing with Mozart.

Then there was a sudden silence which she took for a pause in the music as she switched off the water and stepped out of the shower, to turn at what sounded like a sharply indrawn breath.

Miranda blinked and swallowed, but there was no mistaking Nicholas Barrett standing in the doorway with an expression of arrested wrath on his even features.

CHAPTER FOUR

SHE stood frozen for what seemed like an age but was in fact only a moment, and then with a muttered, 'Oh my God!' jumped back into the shower because there didn't seem to be a towel within reach.

'What the bloody hell's going on?' Nicholas demanded, and strolled further into the bathroom.

Miranda clutched the shower curtain around her. 'I . . . I was playing a record,' she stammered, and drew a breath as he came closer and seemed to tower over her alarmingly.

'Oh, were you? As a matter of fact that was obvious,' he said ironically, and they stared at each other for a long moment.

He must have been sailing or something, she thought irrelevantly as she took in his damp denim shorts and untamed hair. She wrenched her eyes from his narrow waist, flat torso and long powerful legs and said the first thing that came to mind, 'I'm really sorry—I should have asked first before I used it. Do you . . . could you get me a towel?' She looked around wildly and realised there were none in the bathroom. She shut her eyes in furious exasperation. Of course, she'd put the towels in the wash and had been going to put fresh ones out after she'd tidied the guest bathroom. 'From the linen closet?' she added meekly, going hot and cold under his eyes and trying to arrange the shower curtain so that it was more concealing and at the same time hoping desperately that he didn't notice the glass of sherry on the dressing table.

But almost as if reading her thoughts he picked up

the little glass and sniffed at it.

'Sherry?' he queried.

She nodded miserably. 'But only cooking sherry.'

'Well, well,' he said slowly, and put the glass back. 'Miss Smith has decided to live it up a little, has she? Take a few liberties. How many . . . cooking sherries have you had?'

'It's the only one,' she said stiffly, 'and I've only had a sip of it. I'm not drunk, if that's what you're thinking, and I didn't intend to get drunk,' she added more tartly than she'd intended. And then was goaded to more than tartness by the look of mocking amusement in his eyes.

'Is it such a crime?' she cried. 'One little glass of sherry to . . . to . . .' She stopped. 'Oh, I don't know why I had it!' she went on crossly, 'but you can take it out of my wages if you like. And if I damaged the record or the record player you can deduct that too.' She stopped short again and with the utmost clarity recalled *Wuthering Heights* lying open and face down on his desk.

She breathed deeply, knowing full well she was in the wrong on all counts. But somehow, grovelling to this man seemed to be more than she could do, especially as suddenly, like a movie sliding across her mind, she remembered with a vivid startling clarity what he had said to the police prosecutor about her.

It was like a thorn in her flesh that spurred her on. 'I hope you're not going to be your usual superior self over this, Mr Barrett,' she said haughtily, 'because if you are, you might find yourself cooking your own dinner!'

He looked down at her meditatively and with a curious detachment—a look that filled her with some trepidation and made her suddenly regret her impetuous words.

Then he reached out lazily and flicked the shower curtain away from her clutching hands.

'W-what are you doing?' she stammered, trying ineffectually to cover herself with her hands and feeling as if her whole body was blushing.

'Taking a few liberties,' he murmured with a wry look. 'Do you mind?' he asked with the same irony he had used earlier as he reached across leisurely and put her hands at her sides.

Miranda clenched her fists and thought fleetingly of resisting him, but she immediately remembered the ease with which he had overpowered her on that never-to-be-forgotten morning not so long ago.

'Very wise,' he drawled, again reading her thoughts. 'Besides, it would be a shame to put a bruise on such a beautiful body,' he murmured, trailing his fingers around the base of her throat and then flicking the wet ends of her hair back.

She trembled beneath his touch, but she didn't, found she couldn't move away. She also found she was having some difficulty with her breathing, each breath coming as if she'd been running as those roving fingers moved downwards about her breasts, plucking at her nipples very gently until they flowered beneath his hands, bringing a cool, absent smile to his lips as he studied her hot, stunned face.

She lowered her head in an agony of confusion and shame, knowing full well that she had deliberately provoked him at the same time as she had known, from the minute she had laid eyes on him, he wasn't the kind of man you provoked lightly.

She panicked then and took a step backwards, to stumble and slip until he steadied her with his hands about her waist and a wry twist to his lips as he said very quietly, 'I don't know about shorthand-typing and I suppose I'll find out about your culinary expertise a little later, but I think you've missed your calling, Miranda. There's one thing you were made for.'

She closed her eyes and let her head droop at the cruelty of his words. And she knew he was laughing at her, felt it through his hands as they slid from her waist to the swell of her hips. She was thankful for it because it gave her the strength of will to resist the strange, beautiful, tingling lethargy that had invaded her limbs.

'All right,' she whispered, and made herself look up at him. 'I asked for it,' she acknowledged. 'I was in the wrong and I shouldn't have been prickly and defensive about it. I'm sorry.'

For a brief instant she thought she detected a gleam of surprise in his dark eyes, but they narrowed almost immediately and she felt she must have been mistaken.

He said, as he dropped his hands and moved back, 'That's better. You see, it's not that I mind you playing records or imbibing a drop of Dutch courage so long as you don't blast the whole neighbourhood with the noise or get tipsy. Also,' he added as he neatly emptied the sherry glass into the basin, 'if you're going to be hanged for a lamb, you might as well make it a sheep. I have a very fine cream sherry in the cocktail cabinet. Stay where you are,' he added over his shoulder, and walked out with the sherry glass.

Miranda stayed. As if rooted to the spot and several moments later he reappeared with a large fluffy towel and another glass of sherry.

'Try this one,' Nicholas said gravely but with lurking laughter in his eyes as he handed her the glass first and then the towel. 'You'll find it an improvement, I'm sure. Whatever it is you're cooking smells delicious, by the way,' he added, and walked out closing the door behind him.

But it was some time before Miranda moved, and

when she did at last it was with jerky, unco-ordinated movements for a time, which exactly matched her state of mind. And when she finally managed to pull herself together it was to think rather bitterly of Shirley Tate.

'How smug you must have seemed to her, Miranda,' she taunted herself. 'But what price your smugness now?'

By the time she was dressed, though, some of her spirit had returned. Enough, at least, to feel she had been rather shabbily dealt with despite the error of her ways. But she had to keep setting her teeth as she thought of her mute yet undeniable responses to Nicholas.

'Why couldn't I have just stood like a marble statue?' she muttered angrily to herself as she brushed her hair and looped her mother's polished sea-green beads around her neck. Each tiny bead head was carved like a flower and it did look good against her new dress, she noted angrily. In fact the whole image wasn't unpleasing. Her hair shone and her eyes sparked green fire, the dress looked just as good as it had in the shop. But none of this, she thought, can help me go out there and meet him again without curling up and dying of embarrassment! Why, oh, why did I do it? But more to the point, why the hell did he have to come home two hours early?

She flung her brush down angrily and marched into the kitchen, her head held high as she adjusted her apron.

But she didn't encounter her employer until she went to set the table, and when she did she merely ignored his eyes.

'Oh, come on, Miranda!' he said as he followed her into the dining room with a slight grin.

She glanced at him briefly then across the table and noted that he had showered himself and changed into well fitting grey trousers and a black shirt that he was still buttoning up. For some reason this didn't exactly improve her disposition either and she turned away deliberately.

He came round the table and tilted her head up with a finger beneath her chin. 'Anyone would think I'd raped you,' he drawled, and touched the corner of her mouth which was set in a hard line. 'Let's just say we're both a little . . . hot-tempered.'

If that was hot temper I'd hate to see what a blinding rage is, Miranda thought with an inward shiver.

But she said, 'All right. Would you mind getting out of my way, please? Because you see,' she added candidly as she shot him a clear, piercing look from her green eyes, 'I intend to show you tonight one of the things I can do particularly well that isn't—that isn't . . .' she hesitated.

'I understand,' he interrupted gravely but with a glint in his eyes. 'You don't have to spell it out. Would you like me to help you choose the wine for your pièce de résistance?'

She shrugged. 'If you like. Mr Wright always used to do that. He was a bit of a connoisseur. I don't know much about it.'

'Well, I'll teach you,' he said, and took her hand.

Miranda looked down at her hand in his. She could smell the faint tang of his aftershave and was very conscious of his proximity and the strange effect it was having on her. Her hand felt weightless but her arm curiously heavy and her heart was beating lightly and hurriedly somewhere up near her throat. She looked up and could tell by the faint quirk at the corners of his well cut lips that he knew exactly how the close contact woth him was affecting her once more. If I didn't know better, she thought dazedly, I would think he was deliberately . . . pursuing me. But that's *crazy*!

We were talking about wine, not anything else.

She drew a deep breath and with a barely perceptible shake of her head, took her hand away and forced herself to say lightly, 'Okay. Lay on, Macduff. My mother used to read Shakespeare to me,' she added to his faint look of surprise. 'That's how I came to be called Miranda. She was reading *The Tempest* when I was born.'

But although her words were light, she felt a tiny spurt of irritation. Does he honestly think all the readers and thinkers and people who enjoy music and painting and poetry reside only in capital cities? she thought crossly.

His voice interrupted her thoughts. 'Sounds like appropriate reading at a time like that.' He grinned down at her. 'But just think, if she'd been reading *Wuthering Heights*, say, you could have ended up with the much more common name of Cathy.'

Miranda coloured and bit her lip. Sprung yet again! she thought. It's just not my day. And the irritation deepened. 'If your mother had read at a time like that, just think, you could have ended up being called Heathcliff—a much worse fate than Miranda.'

He laughed. 'What a thought! I don't think I'd have enjoyed that at all.'

'But you'd make good Heathcliff,' she said innocently.

He narrowed his eyes and glinted her a look of sheer devilry. 'Touché,' he said softly as she began to regret her words. 'Welcome to the jungle, Miranda. You learn fast. No,' he said as she moved her hands helplessly, 'don't try and change it. Let's just say we're square for the moment. And while you work that one out,' he added very quietly, 'shall we choose the wine?'

It ran through her mind on and off throughout the

dinner party and she wondered why it made her shiver to think of it . . . When you work that one out.

She thought of it as she basted the vegetables and served the soup. It was there as she was briefly introduced to his guests, including his sister Sarah, who was a ravishing brunette and didn't seem to bear any outward marks of her moral degeneration. Of the six other people present, two were a couple with a young baby who very obligingly fell asleep in his carrycot in the guest room, a strikingly handsome middle-aged couple and a man and a woman who appeared not to be attached to anyone. But by the time Miranda had served the pavlova to the tune of warm compliments, she had worked out that the man was with Sarah and the coolly elegant woman with the red-gold hair had a sort of delicately proprietorial attitude towards her host.

This impression was reinforced, Miranda found, back in the kitchen now, but still able to hear the snatches of conversation.

'Heavens!' This was Sarah. 'Can she ever cook! Where did you find—Miranda, is it, Nick?'

'She found me,' Miranda heard her employer say, and could just picture his faintly ironic grin. 'Do you approve, Samantha?' she heard him add.

Samantha. That was her name. The woman with the stunning hair and such an air of poise. And a husky voice she noted as she listened.

'. . . I approve wholeheartedly of this delicious pavlova, Nick darling. You've found yourself a real treasure. How come I haven't met her before?'

I wonder, Miranda mused as the level of conversation fell and her mind's eye turned as if pulled by invisible strings to that blonde nylon negligee that had hung behind the bathroom door.

She rearranged the bowl of fresh fruit and the cheese board she had prepared for anyone without a sweet tooth. She placed them on the trolley next to the coffee percolator and wheeled it through to the dining room.

To arrive just in time to see Samantha place her beautifully manicured hand over Nicholas Barrett's as it lay on the table and smile intimately up into his eyes.

Back once more in the kitchen, Miranda closed the door gently behind her and leant against it with her heart beating a strange tattoo.

Finally she pushed herself away from the door with both hands and surveyed the mild disarray of the kitchen with puzzled eyes as if not quite seeing it. Then she bit her knuckles in exasperation and began stacking the dishwasher. 'This is fast becoming the longest day of my life,' she told the inanimate machine. 'The sooner I get home to bed the better! I'm beginning to think in circles.'

The circles of her mind plagued her for several days to come, though. On Sunday, she persistently mixed up the orders at the take-away until her boss demanded to know what the hell was the matter.

'Nothing,' she said hastily. 'I mustn't have been listening.'

'Well, listen—start listening, will you! I got a shop full of people out there all champing at the bit. And I don't buy this nothing wrong business, because it's just not like you, Miranda!'

Her shorthand class on Monday evening followed a similar pattern.

'Would you read that back, please, Miss Smith?'

Miranda jumped and looked down at the meaningless squiggles on her pad. 'Um . . . er . . .'

'It was basically about concrete specifications for a bridge,' the teacher supplied a little acidly.

'Oh yes. Er . . . the cement shall be . . .' She broke

off helplessly. 'I'm sorry,' she said gruffly, 'I'm a little distracted tonight.'

'That's obvious,' the teacher said not quite kindly, and passed on. She didn't bother Miranda again during the lesson.

When Miranda got home she dropped her armful of books disgustedly to the table and wearily made herself a cup of tea. A light breeze was finally lifting the heavy humidity that characterised Brisbane in midsummer and she pulled her armchair forward to the window and let it blow over her gratefully and cool her over-heated skin as it billowed the curtains inward. The night was dark and quiet now.

She sipped her tea and forced herself to analyse her thoughts.

I can't go on like this, she told herself. And just what am I going on about anyway? One man? A man I have every reason to hate, what's more.

She sighed and pulled at a loose thread on the arm of the chair. Then she set her lips mutinously and wondered if she'd ever forget standing stark naked in that bathroom. Or what had followed.

'Or what followed.' She made herself say the words out loud. 'That's where the problem lies. I think, incredible as it seems, Miranda, you have to admit you're a little attracted to Nicholas Barrett, Q.C.'

She stood up impatiently. '*All right! So what if I am? He's an incredibly attractive man. That doesn't mean to say he's likeable.*'

But isn't he? an inner voice prompted. If you forget about what he said about you when he didn't even know you, and remember that he did burst in on you playing his records, drinking his sherry, reading his book and then being defiant about it—if you wipe all that out, can you say you don't like him? That you don't find him the most mentally challenging person you've ever been with? And even if you can't forget all the rest, isn't it all part of the attraction anyway?

She shivered suddenly and sat down again and examined the thought that had made her shiver in the first place. While she might find Nicholas mentally as well as physically attractive, wouldn't it be supremely foolish to imagine that he would return the compliment on both counts? Perhaps the physical part, but would he ever imagine she could match his mind? She grimaced to herself. He had only ever indicated the exact opposite if anything.

She sighed again and leant her head back tiredly. And all of a sudden was washed by a terrible tide of homesickness. If only she had someone to confide in! If only she could be with them—just that would help immensely. She thought of Bill Hartley. Bill, who loved her with a deep, steady love that warmed her through and through and had, for her at least, had none of this kind of uncertainty. She knew he loved her. She knew she loved him—in a way. And in her heart of hearts she expected to go back to that deep, steady flame once she had got this restlessness out of her soul.

So, if this was true, why was she in such a state now? Why couldn't she just laugh off this business with Nicholas Barrett as she had with the vet she'd 'fallen in love with' and mooned over several years ago when she thought he wasn't looking? Or the relieving minister who had taken her fancy for those couple of months so that she went to church more regularly than she ever had in her life before, until she had realised that every female member of the congregation from eight to eighty had felt the same?

She smiled faintly. 'He was lovely,' she murmured reminiscently. 'And so serious, and if anyone needed a wife, he did.'

But she sobered, dismally aware that what she was experiencing now wasn't quite in the same category. It was one thing to weave fanciful daydreams about someone who wasn't really aware of your existence, but quite another to be in close contact with someone like Nicholas Barrett ...

She closed her eyes and thought, but how to equate this with Bill? I've been thinking of my youthful peccadilloes—or wishful ones, rather, but I've never before encountered something that's set me to this level of introspection. Oh, Mum, I need you now!

Curiously, it was the thought of her mother that calmed Miranda. I'm letting my imagination run away with me, she told herself. I'm building great castles out of *nothing*! He probably has exactly the same way about him with every passable female he meets. It's probably second nature but just a bit more effective because I'm ... well, Miranda Smith, lately come to the big city, perhaps a bit more naïve than most.

'And that is that!' She said it out aloud and stood up and began determinedly to prepare for bed, refusing to allow herself to indulge in any more soul-searching.

CHAPTER FIVE

THE next two weeks, however, lulled her strange fancies and curious notions, she found. She didn't lay eyes on Nick Barrett, and the odd feeling that she was playing a dangerous game just by being in his apartment subsided somewhat. The only communication she had from him was in the form of a brief note congratulating her on the success of her meal. All very proper except for the postscript. The note had been propped beside a book on his desk and the postscript said, 'If you haven't already finished the book, please feel free to borrow it.' It was *Wuthering Heights*.

Miranda grimaced wryly to herself, but nevertheless went home with it.

Then, three weeks after the dinner, she got a phone call from Mrs Marshall in the apartment on Thursday morning.

They exchanged pleasantries until Mrs Marshall said, 'I do hope you've forgiven me for what I did, Miranda?'

'Did?' Miranda queried after a moment.

'Yes. You see, when you came to me for that interview, I recognised you from our dear mutual employer's description of a certain court case he'd attended.'

'He told you about it?' Miranda said incredulously.

'He did. And if there's one thing I can't abide it's smug, superior men.'

'But . . . but . . .' Miranda spluttered. 'I mean, why did you do it?'

'Because I was a country girl myself once, Miranda,'

Mrs Marshall said gently. 'And when they know that it's like an invisible brand you have to wear. So I decided to take a punt on you, that you could show him there was more to you than he assumed. And it seemed it paid off, my dear. Not that he's ever extravagant in his praise but I gather between the lines he's very pleased with you and not quite so smug about . . .' She hesitated.

'About buxom bushies?' Miranda supplied gently.

'Exactly,' Mrs Marshall agreed, and they both laughed. 'But to get back to business, Miranda, it's Sarah's birthday tomorrow week and the idea of a surprise birthday party has come up. Mr Barrett wondered if you'd care to take on the catering?'

'Well, how many people, and what kind of food did he have in mind?' Miranda asked, her mind suddenly buzzing.

'It seems it's Samantha Seymour's idea,' Mrs Marshall said in a slightly altered voice. 'If you took it on you'd have to consult with her. She has carte blanche, I gather.'

Now I wonder why Mrs Marshall doesn't approve of Samantha Seymour, Miranda thought. Or is it my imagination?

'All right,' she said into the phone. 'At least, I'll discuss it with her,' she added, and feeling an inward tremor of excitement, 'perhaps I *could* make a business out of this.'

'Well, why don't I arrange for her to come and see you at the apartment on Saturday morning? When you're there at work again?'

'That sounds fine, Mrs Marshall. And thank you for taking a punt on me.'

'My pleasure, Miranda . . .'

Saturday zoomed round so that the intervening hours

seemed like a telescoped movie to Miranda as she sat opposite Samantha Seymour in Nicholas Barrett's lounge and was a little surprised to find that Samantha looked younger than she remembered. Not quite so much the elegant woman of the world, although she was faultlessly dressed in a split khaki skirt and a buttercup yellow blouse. Perhaps it was because that glorious red-gold hair was lying loose today.

Samantha smiled at her easily and said, 'Do you know, I'm dying for a cup of coffee. I seem to have been rushing since I got up!'

Miranda stood up. 'Of course. I feel a little the same myself. It won't take a minute.'

But her companion rose gracefully and followed her into the kitchen.

'You keep this place so perfect,' she commented as she trailed her fingertips across the gleaming white counter top. 'If ever Nick lets you go, do come and see me won't you? I could always use you.'

Miranda digested this in silence as she prepared the coffee and decided she didn't quite like it. It's as if I've been rather delicately put in my place. But then again, I suppose it is my place, she thought with a rueful grin and an inward shrug.

She said, 'How many people did you have in mind for this party, Miss Seymour?'

'I've thought of fifty,' said Samantha in her attractive gravelly voice.

Miranda blanched. 'F-fifty?' she stammered.

'Mmm,' Samantha agreed. 'That's just a nice number to make it interesting, and Nick's got the space to accommodate them. You could fit a small flat into his lounge alone, couldn't you?' She went on without waiting for Miranda to reply. 'I thought of a buffet supper, later in the evening, and a birthday cake, and to keep them happy until then some sustaining snacks.'

She looked at Miranda expectantly.

'It would take an lot of preparation,' Miranda said at last. 'And I'm not an expert at cake icing and decorating. But,' she said with sudden decision, 'I'd do the rest. Perhaps you could order the cake from a confectioner?'

Samantha nodded and hesitated. 'Could you make the food rather special, Miranda?' she asked with a suddenly thoughtful look. 'Or perhaps I should make out a menu?'

Miranda shrugged. 'If you want to. But I wasn't planning a chicken and chips and cheerios kind of do. The other thing is, plates and glasses. Will there be enough?'

'I'd thought of that. I'll be bringing some over. I . . . I did have something else in mind, Miranda. I have a maid's uniform at home, you know the kind of thing, black dress, frilly white apron and cap. It would—well, it would save your own clothes, wouldn't it? I thought it would be rather suitable.'

Well, *I* don't, Miranda said, but beneath her breath before she swung round to shoot Samantha Seymour a clear green, piercing glance. But she spoke quite gently. 'Thank you for your concern, Miss Seymour, for my clothes. But I think I'd feel a little uncomfortable looking like something out of *Upstairs, Downstairs*. Your coffee,' she added smoothly, and passed a cup and saucer down the counter.

'Oh dear!' said Samantha with her thin pencilled eyebrows raised, 'I didn't mean to upset you, Miranda. Please wear whatever you like.'

'You didn't,' Miranda said calmly, and with some disregard for the truth. 'Is there anything else?'

'I don't think so.' Samantha glanced at her watch. 'Oh! How time has flown! I do really have to dash. Look, I'll leave it all to you, Miranda, but if you have

any problems, give me a ring. Sorry about the coffee
. . .' And she was gone.

Miranda stared at the empty doorway with narrowed
eyes and thought, no wonder Mrs Marshall doesn't like
her! She's a right . . .! She bit her tongue and then
forced herself to relax. I'll give her a maid's uniform,
she thought. I'll prepare the best darn party fare she's
ever had!

But on the day before the party as she set out to work,
she was experiencing severe qualms herself. She'd
planned to spend the whole day doing as much of the
advance cooking as she could, but she found she dearly
wished she had someone to talk to about it all. Samantha
had left her severely alone since their first discussion
and her only communication with her employer had
been in the form of another note telling her he'd made
arrangements for her to charge all her marketing to
him.

'I'd just like to see him once before the party,
though,' she muttered to herself as she inserted her
key into the doorway of number forty-five.

She closed the door behind her and jumped as an
inner door opened.

'Who's there?' she called as she swung round.

'Who do you think?' a deep, sarcastic voice replied.

'Oh, Mr Barrett!' she exclaimed as she took in the
tall figure leaning against the lounge doorway. 'You
made me jump! I was just thinking of you, as a matter
of fact.' She spoke hastily and a little unevenly.

'How odd, Miranda,' Nicholas Barrett answered
without straightening up. 'I was thinking of you.
Perhaps we should compare notes?' he added casually
as his dark eyes flicked over her with a curious glint in
them.

Miranda swallowed and thought dazedly, only a

month since I last saw him. Only four short weeks, but I feel now as if I've been dying of thirst and stumbled across a waterhole in the Simpson Desert. She lowered her head as their eyes met, but it was all there in her mind like a glossy print—how he seemed taller than she remembered, the way his dark hair fell, the clever chiselled lines of his features, the strength and elegance of his beautifully made body which none of his clothes hid. All there like a blow to her heart.

She made herself look up again to find his scrutiny hadn't altered, and frowned faintly as she realised he didn't look quite normal. Less than immaculate, she noted. He wore a severely tailored dark suit and blue silk shirt, but his tie was loosened and his hair ruffled as if he'd pulled his hand through it. And then there was the unnerving way he was looking at her as if he was testing his memory of her.

She asked, 'Are you all right? You don't look . . .' She tailed off helplessly and rubbed her palms together awkwardly as she gazed at him with real concern now.

He straightened up then and raised his eyebrows. 'Miranda, come to bed with me. I think we both want it.' His voice was even and the words unhurried, and there was no mistaking them or the feel of his fingers on her wrist as he reached out a hand to fiddle absently with the narrow silver bangle she wore.

Miranda closed her mouth with a click and wondered wildly what to say. She looked round the dim cool vestibule and licked her lips. 'I couldn't do that, Mr Barrett,' she said, her voice hoarse and uncertain. She felt herself break out into a cold sweat because the words sounded inane and foolish and she wished she'd just said no. Then she made an effort to collect herself. 'I think you're just trying to shock me,' she went on. 'I'm sure you didn't really mean it . . .'

'But I did, Miranda,' he interrupted.

She stared up at him and felt herself go strangely weak at the knees and hot and cold by turns because although his words had sounded detached almost, there was nothing detached about the way he was looking at her.

'I usually do mean what I say,' his mouth twisted wryly, 'and I've wanted to do this for some time.'

He pulled at her bangle gently, but she resisted the pressure, refusing to allow herself to be pulled into his arms with the incredible turmoil of her mind etched plainly on her face.

They stood like that for what seemed like an eternity, the only point of contact between them the bangle on her outstretched arm. Then he dropped her arm and moved forward himself.

She backed away, but was brought up almost immediately by the front door behind her which brought a sudden gleam of amusement to his intent dark eyes and she froze as he reached out again, this time with both hands to cup her shoulders and spread his fingers gently beneath the material of her sleeveless dress.

Miranda found her tongue again. 'No,' she whispered gently. 'No, please!'

'Miranda,' he said after a moment, 'look, we could dress this up and play a lot of silly games. We could give it a variety of names which have lost all meaning. Or we could be realistic about it and admit, as I do now, that I've wanted you since I caught you in the shower . . .'

She trembled beneath his hands and felt them tighten momentarily.

'Yes,' he said dryly, 'it's as simple as that. And if I'd gone on playing the right cards that afternoon you'd have slept with me there and then.'

Miranda closed her eyes and tried desperately to think—and in her desperation said the words she would have despised if they'd come from someone else. 'Why me? I didn't think I was your sort.'

He grimaced. 'You're very much my sort at the moment, my dear. I notice you haven't attempted to deny my ... assumption about that afternoon.' He looked at her searchingly.

She dropped her eyes miserably. 'I don't know,' she said helplessly. Her voice lowered. 'But I can't do this,' she added, and tensed as he ran his hands slowly and caressingly up and down her upper arms.

'Why not, Miranda?' he said quietly. 'Believe me, it's going to come to this with some man sooner than you think. You remind me of an exotic blossom that's been flowering somewhere unnoticed, just waiting to be discovered. And, with some help along the road you've already begun to tread, you could go anywhere, Miranda. Realise all those dreams I know you have locked in your heart.'

'C-can't I do that on my own?' she stammered, and knew it wasn't what she should be saying.

'Maybe,' Nick said expressionlessly, and let his eyes roam her face and lips. 'But this way would be a lot quicker and a lot more fun,' he added with his lips barely moving.

Something stirred beneath Miranda's drugged senses. Something that intruded beyond the fact that her skin under his hands had seemed to have broken out in a fine enchanted trembling as if it had a life of its own. Something that pulled her back from the brink she felt she was teetering on.

Her eyes widened incredulously as that something crystallised in her mind. 'You're bartering with me, aren't you?' she whispered.

'I wouldn't have put it like that ...'

'But it's the same thing,' she said, her voice rising and falling unevenly. 'In exchange for a few short weeks of my body—until you get me out of your system, I get some sort of entrée into *your* world—I'm surprised you don't come out and name a figure. Just tell me one thing,' she demanded, going rigid in his arms which had slipped right round her, 'what kind of a label will stick on me when you've done with me? How about— Been to Finishing School. Or—Second-hand but well run in? That's a good one. Do you think I'll be allowed off the grass then?'

She saw the frown of recognition that came to his eyes.

'Oh yes, I heard it all,' she said through her teeth. 'I was very definitely not your type then, wasn't I? Well, I'm *still* not. Perhaps you were right after all—you and the police prosecutor. Maybe I am only a dim, little twit from the country, but that's the way I plan to stay, so you'll have to look somewhere else for your little bit of fun . . . you were a fine one to preach about wolves in sheep's clothing!'

'Miranda . . .'

'Don't Miranda me,' she said contemptuously. 'I'm not *that* lonely or that desperate. As a matter of fact I quite like myself the way I am. So thank you, kind sir, but the answer's no! No!' she sobbed as the tears streamed down her face.

'I heard you the first time,' Nick countered coolly. 'You don't have to shout like a fishwife.'

'Oh!' she gasped, and with a superhuman effort wrenched herself free of his embrace and dealt him a stinging blow on the cheek with her open hand.

He didn't flinch or move away or do anything for a long moment as her hand fell back slackly, but she took a sudden breath as his eyes changed and she realised how effectively she was trapped, still in his reach, still hemmed in.

But he took his time about it. 'There's an old saying

about an eye for an eye, Miranda,' he murmured. 'Have you encountered the Bible in your literary excursions?'

'Yes. *No*,' she breathed as she sought to evade him, but found it impossible. She found she was locked in his arms and then in the split second before he lowered his dark head, saw that hateful light of mockery in his eyes.

It was a brutal, savage kiss that hurt her bottom lip and frightened her to a mindless, strengthless resistance as easily overpowered as if she was somehow boneless. But it changed imperceptibly as she gave up the unequal struggle and sagged against him as she'd done once before in a submission of defeat. Changed then to an experience of languorous beauty which seemed to involve her whole body, to capture all her senses until she was conscious of nothing but the feel of Nick's body taut and strong against her own and the taste of him like some intoxicating liquor. Changed to a feeling of captivity that longed for the release that would allow her hands the freedom of his body as he had of her.

He raised his head at last and their eyes met, his darkly brooding as they rested on her swollen lips, hers wide and unsure and glittering with unshed tears.

'If that's barter, Miranda,' he said quietly but with an edge of suppressed violence, 'I wonder . . . hell!' he exclaimed violently. 'Don't look like that! It was only a kiss.'

She nodded like a marionette. 'Of course,' she mumbled. 'I'll . . . I think I'll go now.'

His hands fell away. 'Go where?' he queried harshly.

'H-home,' she stuttered, and with a lightning move that seemed to be directed from somewhere outside her body, turned, found the doorhandle beneath her fingers and with a quick twist opened it and slipped through.

It was a nightmare journey home and when she finally got there she sank into her armchair feeling exhausted and drained and unable to think clearly, save for two thoughts that seemed to beat at her brain: I've lost my heart and I've lost my job.

'No, Miranda,' she corrected herself fiercely when her breathing had steadied. She stood up impatiently. 'Your job, yes, but not your heart. It's only a passing fancy, no more surely.'

But the tears welled again until she threw herself on to the bed and sobbed into the pillow.

She didn't hear the knock on the door, but she turned her head as it opened and then jerked upright as Nicholas entered her room and closed the door behind him. Her mouth fell open and for a long moment she gazed at him as he looked round the room coolly and then let his dark eyes rest on her flushed, tear-streaked face.

She exhaled deeply, bitterly aware of how shabby the room would look to him, of how her underwear hanging up to dry in the bathroom was visible through the open doorway and of what a mess she felt and no doubt looked. Then she felt a stiffening of resolution and pulled her hanky from her sleeve to blow her nose.

'I suppose you're worried about your party,' she muttered as she slid off the bed and stood twisting the handkerchief.

He thrust his hands into his pockets and walked across to the window. 'I couldn't give a damn about the party,' he said as he looked out on to the neighbouring yard. He turned. 'I came to talk to you, Miranda. To . . . explain.'

She winced as his sombre eyes travelled over her. 'You don't have to,' she said huskily. 'They say eavesdroppers never hear good of themselves. Anyway, I'm sure you had the whole court in agreement with you.'

He started to say something and then seemed to change his mind. 'Of all people, I should have known better than to jump to such a hasty conclusion, Miranda,' he said quietly, and added, 'I'm sorry about that too, but it isn't only that.'

She stared down at her working fingers and thought miserably that the last thing she wanted was a whole lot of apologies. 'I think it's best if we just forget it.' She looked up and their eyes locked.

'No, I don't think so,' he said at last as his gaze dropped to her still swollen lip. 'I was in a particularly foul mood this morning when you arrived. I'd just heard that a client I'd been instructed to represent on a murder charge had hanged himself. I thought he was the victim of some pretty circumstantial evidence and tended to believe he was innocent as he claimed. When I thought of the despair and lack of faith in justice he must have felt to commit suicide—I'm afraid it rather got to me. And you, unfortunately, turned up at the wrong time. Otherwise I'd have vented my frustration on something . . . inanimate, possibly.'

Miranda blinked and swallowed as she absorbed this. 'I . . . didn't know,' she said haltingly. 'I'm sorry.'

'You couldn't have,' he said abruptly. 'Which makes it less forgivable. I also have a reputation for being moody, as my sister Sarah and Mrs Marshall put it. But you couldn't have known that either. It's probably I, in fact, who deserve a label if anyone does. How does—Beware! He bites, sound?'

He said it very seriously, but she could see the faint smile lurking in his eyes all the same and felt herself relaxing just slightly.

'Prickly,' she said, then coloured. 'I mean, that's what Mrs Marshall said . . .'

'I can imagine,' he interrupted with a grin. 'The voice of my conscience is Mrs Marshall.'

Miranda smiled faintly back at him. She hesitated. 'Well, that explains it, I suppose.'

'Does it?'

'Doesn't it?' she said stupidly. 'I thought it did.'

'Then you thought wrong, Miranda,' Nick said quietly. 'What I was feeling this morning gave me the impetus to lapse into an ego trip you found unacceptable. More so, I now realise, because of what you overheard that day in court. But it doesn't alter the basic . . . attraction that lay between the two of us—I think. I said I couldn't cloak it with any unmeaningful names. But I can't deny its existence. Can you?'

She shivered suddenly because he was watching her carefully, his dark saturnine features alert so that she experienced the curious feeling of being in a witness box again and thought, this is how he would look in court just before he cut me down, tore my inarticulate defences to shreds.

'No,' she said finally, desperately conscious that she had to choose each word with care and somehow make him understand. 'But I have to question it. And not only because of what I overheard. That,' she shrugged, 'well, I could have lived with that. But you see, I've been attracted . . . I've felt like this a couple of times before.'

She swallowed and contemplated her hands as she sought for the right words. She looked up at last and said painfully, 'It comes and goes, though, doesn't it? But my mother and father, they had the real thing. It *does* exist, I know, because I saw it with my own eyes. They didn't have it easy, but they didn't care because they had each other. They were so different, but he cared for her more than anything in this world. And for her, he was her whole life. If,' she hesitated, 'if I did go to any man, I'd want to at least *think* at the time I was going for broke. Like they did. I know it probably seems crazy to you and I'm glad you didn't try and call it by any names it wasn't, string me any false lines. But I just couldn't do it . . . this way.'

The only sound that disturbed the sudden silence was the putt-putting of a lawnmower down the street.

'I see,' Nick said finally, and Miranda searched his face desperately, but all she could find was some compassion that she interpreted as being felt for her, being caught in yet another impossibly awkward situation. And the tiny seed of hope that had sprouted unbidden in her heart died. But you knew it was always a lost cause, didn't you, Miranda? she thought, and turned away feeling inexpressibly sad.

Then she made an effort to collect herself and spoke without thinking as she turned back, 'On the other hand,' she said, trying to sound lighthearted, 'I know it sounds silly, but you've given my confidence a bit of a boost. Quite wiped out what you said that day.' She managed to smile at him.

He stared at her with lifted eyebrows and a reluctant grin tugging at the corners of his lips. 'It was an honour,' he said gently.

'Do you want me to come back? I'd understand if you didn't. Or maybe after the party . . .?' She lifted her shoulders in irritation at her own hastily spoken words that had bubbled out after the unbearable tension of the moment.

'Miranda, I didn't come to see you because I was in any way concerned with this damn party. To be honest I'm not even sure if it's a very good idea.' He looked suddenly impatient.

'I know that,' she said slowly.

'Well then, if you'd like to come back to work for me, I'd be very happy to have you.' He smiled crookedly.

'If you think you can put up with me. But as for to-morrow night,' he said more soberly, and looked at her searchingly, 'particularly if you don't feel up to much today, I could very easily cancel the whole thing.'

'I appreciate that,' she said quietly, and took a deep breath. 'But I said I'd do it so I ought to. I did think—well, I thought I might be able to . . . make a business out of this kind of thing. I'd still finish my secretarial course, but perhaps there are possibilities? If people got to know me.'

She eyed him uncertainly, vividly recalling their Duchess of Duke Street conversation and wondering if he'd laugh at her this time.

But he surprised her again. He said very gently, 'If you were calling for investors, Miranda, I'd back you to the hilt. In fact if there's anything I can do to start the ball rolling, I will.'

She blushed with pleasure. 'Thank you.' She glanced at her watch, and winced. 'If I'm not going to damage my reputation before I even get started, I should get back to work!'

CHAPTER SIX

MIRANDA took a deep breath and surveyed the utter chaos in Nicholas Barrett's kitchen. She closed the door and leant back against it wearily. The party was in full swing and she had just served the buffet supper. She rubbed her temples with her forefingers and sent up a little prayer that the food was all right, because the truth to tell she had found that despite her hours of preparation, the scale of this party had tested her to the limit.

And all those exotic dishes, she thought wearily, as she pushed herself away from the door. I do hope they taste all right. And just look at this mess!

She closed her eyes instead and took another deep breath. And grimaced wryly as she opened them again and found it hadn't gone away.

'O.K, just take it steady, Miranda,' she murmured to herself.

She stacked the dishwasher and set out to do the remainder by hand, refusing to allow herself to think of all the dishes still to be done, not to mention the glasses as well.

'I could still be here by sunrise,' she muttered, and found the thought rather alarmingly, so she quickened her tempo and switched her thoughts to the party and the guests as she washed and dried.

Samantha had arrived early and insisted on setting the buffet table and decorating it herself. Miranda had wanted to object, because she had planned to decorate it, but in the last-minute rush she had found herself in, she hadn't had the time. And besides, she had found herself a little daunted by the sight of Samantha in a bewitching gold harem suit with her red-gold hair piled on top of her head and the unmistakable glint of admiration in Nicholas Barrett's eyes whenever they rested on her.

Miranda stopped washing for a moment and thought back to the last half hour before the party had started. Samantha and Nick had enjoyed a quiet drink together seated side by side on the window seat with only one lamp illuminating the room dimly and the stars and lights of Brisbane and the river behind them.

They had made a stunning picture, and Miranda had caught her breath as she had crossed the room quietly with a tray in her hands. They hadn't heard, or if they had, they hadn't taken any notice of her. Her employer wore a lightweight grey suit tonight with a midnight blue shirt and he had been looking out across the river. But as Miranda had passed he had turned his head at something Samantha had said and grinned at her in acknowledgement of her remark, then let his dark eyes roam over the golden harem suit and back up to rest on Samantha's face. And Miranda had stumbled with her tray and gone hot and cold as he lifted his eyes to hers and raised one eyebrow ironically.

She had removed herself with all haste and when she had got back to the kitchen had berated herself roundly as she had tried to identify exactly what it was she had felt in that moment as she had watched him look at Samantha.

It *was* jealousy, she thought now as she plunged her hands back into the soapy water. And a curious feeling of hurt that he should have got over her so quickly. She smiled at her thoughts.

'What's to get over?' she murmured to herself with a shrug. 'He saw me with no clothes on and decided he wanted to take me to bed. Because I refused, do I

expect him to pine away with unrequited love or desire
. . . or whatever it is? Oh no,' she told herself. 'In fact
I should be happy, because he was really very decent
about it all once he . . .' She broke off and sighed.
'Forget about it, Miranda. Just . . . forget it. We both
said all there was to say.'

She deliberately transferred her thoughts to the
dishes and again quickened her tempo. And started to
think of his sister Sarah . . .

Sarah Barrett had apparently arrived this evening to
what she had thought was going to be a small birthday
dinner. She had come unescorted, and to Miranda's
eyes, as she had unashamedly peeped round the kitchen
door, she had looked tired and unhappy. Nick had
greeted her and for a moment Miranda had been struck
by the similarity between the two and also the sudden
look of concern in her employer's eyes as he had
greeted his sister. She remembered how he had said he
wasn't at all sure if this party was a good idea, and saw
him hesitate as he took in the dark circles under Sarah's
eyes. But a moment later, the still, quiet apartment
had erupted into a blaze of light and sound and a
chorus of Surprise! Surprise!

And Sarah had been surprised and she had hesitated
too, Miranda had noted, before being deluged beneath
a welter of affectionate embraces and greetings. But
from then on she had entered into the spirit of the
party with zest.

'Too much zest?'

Miranda pondered her words and decided she was
imagining things. Imagining that there was an un-
natural glitter in Sarah Barrett's beautiful dark eyes
and an invisible air of strain about her.

'How would I know anyway?' she asked herself as
she moved about the kitchen putting things away. 'I've
barely met her. But she's the only one of that mob out

there,' she tossed her head in the direction of the lounge that was now throbbing with music, 'who could be bothered to put her head round the kitchen door and see how I was going! For all Miss Samantha Seymour cares I could be a . . . slave!'

She shut a cupboard sharply and then had the grace to laugh at herself. 'A very well paid slave,' she reminded herself. 'So why should I care if she treats me like some dim little serving maid?'

She worked on, determinedly shutting her thoughts down, and finally she had restored some kind of order to the kitchen and had just brewed herself a cup of tea and was wondering whether they had finished eating out there when an unbidden thought strayed into her mind.

She set her cup down carefully and examined it. Did the likeness between Sarah Barrett and her brother extend to their mental processes? she wondered. Because if they did she had the same feeling that Sarah was as disturbed this evening as her brother had been on the morning when he had offered to take her to bed.

'That's what she reminds me of,' she told herself quietly as she sipped her tea again. 'There's the same air of . . . tension, somehow . . .'

She stared unseeingly across the kitchen for several moments and then gave herself a little shake. It was none of her business anyway. She slipped off the kitchen stool and decided it was time to investigate how her food had gone down.

She found that the lights in the lounge had been dimmed and that apart from odd groups scattered around most of the partygoers were dancing. She paused for a moment in the shadows on her way across to the dining room. The music wasn't particularly loud, but the magnificent stereo speakers seemed to

make the sound throb and the beat of the music insid-
uously inviting so that she longed to be out there herself abandoning her body languorously to it. She closed
her eyes and by some unkind trick of her imagination,
pictured herself in Nicholas's arms, moving against
him in time to the music.

She opened her eyes impatiently to see Samantha
Seymour doing just that, her red-gold head tilted back
as she gazed up into her partner's dark eyes.

Miranda moved restlessly and slipped into the
dining room.

It seemed her food had been a success, she noted as
she ran her eye over the table. There wasn't much left
anyway, and she busied herself collecting the empty
dishes and plates and stacking them on the trolley. A
few people drifted into the dining room and then, realising who she was, congratulated her warmly.

It wasn't until she'd made several trips and almost
cleared the table that she was struck by another unbidden thought. In those trips across the corner of her
lounge she hadn't once seen Sarah, hadn't picked her
out amongst the dancers or anywhere else.

Miranda's busy hands stilled and she felt her heart
beat uncomfortably. Why do I have this strange feeling
about Sarah Barrett? she asked herself. Why?

She pushed the trolley back into the kitchen and
came to a sudden decision. After all, I had the right
instinct about Shirley Tate, didn't I? she thought.

The bedroom area of the apartment was quiet and
deserted. Miranda thought then of the study and
checked it, but it was deserted too. Perhaps she's had
too much to drink, she thought, and retraced her steps
to the main bedroom. The en-suite bathroom door was
ajar, she noticed as she walked right into the room,
with a faint beam of light spilling through. She walked
up to the door, which was out of sight of the main

door, and tapped on it tentatively. There was no response, so she pushed it open, then stifled a strangled cry at what she saw—Sarah slumped on the white-tiled floor with a thin trickle of blood coming from one limp wrist.

Miranda sprang into action. She grabbed a linen hand towel from a rail and bound it round the wrist. Then she gathered Sarah's dark head into her lap and inspected her critically. She brushed the damp tendrils of hair from her brow and felt for her pulse. A very little reassured, she carefully laid Sarah's head back with some towels beneath. Then she stumbled up and hastened into the bedroom, to bump into someone coming in.

It was no one she knew, a middle-aged woman with a careful hair-do.

'I was looking for a toilet . . .'

'Next door on the right,' said Miranda, 'but please do me a favour first. Would you find Mr Barrett and ask him to come here. *Please*,' she entreated, and forcibly turned the lady in the direction of the lounge. 'Tell him Miss Smith would like to see him—at once.'

The lady looked puzzled, then shrugged and wandered off.

Miranda dashed back into the bathroom and knelt down beside Sarah again. The linen towel seemed to be acting effectively and she couldn't think of any more she could do. She bent over the unconscious face and stroked it gently. 'Oh, Sarah, how bad must you have felt to do this! But things can't ever be that bad. You'll see . . .'

'God!'

Miranda turned her head at the muttered expletive and felt a shudder of relief as she saw Nicholas at the bathroom door with Samantha beside him, staring at a

smear of blood on the floor and more on Miranda's
dress.

'Oh dear,' Samantha sighed, 'I can't stand the sight
of blood.' She put a hand to her head in a delicate
gesture, but was pushed unceremoniously aside as Nick
entered the bathroom and knelt down beside Miranda.

'I don't think it's that serious,' Miranda stammered
as he lifted the awkwardly bandaged wrist, his face pale
and beaded with sweat. 'I don't think it happened too
long ago . . .'

'But she's out like a light!'

'Not from loss of blood, though. I think she might
have fainted . . . before she did too much damge. We
should get her to a hospital or a doctor as soon as we
can, though. If you arrange that I'll stay with her.
Don't worry,' she said urgently, 'I'll look after her.'
And she drew the dark head into her lap so that she
could cradle it in her arms.

He stood up and without even glancing at Samantha,
pushed past her again so that she staggered and for no
reason cast Miranda a vicious look of dislike before she
turned on her heel and followed him.

Miranda rode with Nicholas and his sister in the
ambulance and watched as Sarah Barrett was wheeled
through a set of swinging doors. Then she turned to
Sarah's brother.

'She'll be all right. We got to her in time.'

He said violently, 'But why did she do it?'

'Nick,' she used his name unconsciously for the first
time as she took in the anger and pain in his dark eyes,
'you mustn't blame yourself. It . . . just takes some people
this way and there's not a whole lot you can do about it.'

'But I *knew*,' he said in a bitter self-accusing voice.
'Deep down I knew the kind of strain she was under.
And yet I let myself be talked into this party—although
I honestly didn't believe she'd do this. I even,' his

voice thickened, 'Heaven help me, I even felt impatient with her because I could see what an effort she was making. Why the hell can't she just forget him?'

Miranda trembled at the savage way he spoke and unthinkingly moved close to him and put her arm round him as if she was comforting a child. 'Don't . . . you mustn't blame yourself. Anyone with half a mind could see how much you love her.'

He looked down at her. 'And failed her,' he said tightly, and as if it was the most natural, comforting thing in the world, drew her into his arms. 'If only you knew how much I really wanted to help her! But now she's lying there,' he said into her hair, 'lying there . . .'

'She'll be all right. We got to her in time.'

'*You* got to her in time,' he muttered, and gathered her more closely into his arms. 'If it hadn't been for you, she could have died. How did you come to find her?'

'I just had this feeling. I saw the way she looked tonight and after what you'd told me—well, I went to look for her.'

'Thank goodness for you, Miranda,' he said as his arms tightened around her.

They stood like that for minutes. Then she loosened his arms and said gently as she took his hand in hers, 'Come and sit down. I'll see if I can get us a cup of coffee or something.'

'No, I'll do it. You sit down,' he said after a moment during which he visibly took hold of himself. He led her to a chair in the dim waiting room. 'You can't be feeling too good yourself,' he commented dryly as she sank down gratefully and realised just how shaky she did feel. 'Your pretty dress is ruined too,' he went on in the same dry voice, and Miranda looked down at the dress she had bought for his first dinner party.

'It doesn't matter, it's only a dress.'

'I'll buy you a new one.'

She started to say, oh no, when they both started as the waiting room door opened, but it was only a nurse with two cups of coffee for them.

'You must be a mind-reader,' said Nick. 'How is she?'

But the nurse didn't know and for a moment Miranda feared he was going to fling the coffee cup at her in his frustration, but he restrained himself with an effort and the nurse scuttled out rather fearfully.

'Sit down, Nick,' Miranda said soothingly. 'They'll be doing all they can. You shouldn't make it harder for them.'

He sat down beside her and she heard his teeth grind just before he said roughly, 'I phoned a friend of mine, a doctor. He should be here by now!'

'Maybe he is. But anyway, there's a whole team of doctors here.'

'I know that,' he said tautly, 'but he's brilliant.'

'And I'm quite sure everyone here is fully trained to cope with these kind of emergencies,' she countered. 'It's a very big hospital.'

'Miranda,' he ground out, and turned towards her, 'I nearly threw this coffee over that stupid little nurse. I could quite easily do it to you, if you don't stop uttering platitudes!'

Miranda sipped her coffee unperturbed. 'Go ahead,' she said with a faint smile, 'if it makes you feel better. I don't really mind now it's cooled down.'

She looked up at him calmly and saw him take a sudden breath. And his next words jolted her as his offer to pour coffee over her had not.

He said, barely moving his lips, 'Bill Hartley wants his head read, Miranda. He should have taken you to his bed years ago. If I'd have been him I would have. And kept you there.'

'Why . . . why do you say that?' she stammered as she felt her face flame.

Nick studied the colour that came to her cheeks for so long that she thought he wasn't going to answer, at the same time as she felt her treacherous nerve-endings come alive as only he seemed to be able to make them with just a look.

But it was he who broke that long glance first. He set his cup down abruptly and reached out to take her hand in his. Then he said abruptly, 'If I had to go through this, I can't think of any better person to go through it with than you, Miranda. That's what I mean. You're going to make someone a very fine wife and someone's children an equally fine mother. You have an inner strength that doesn't . . . that one doesn't usually associate with those . . . rather voluptuous curves you have.'

His last words had a wry inflection that was echoed in his eyes as he looked at her again.

Miranda grimaced inwardly at the hurt she felt somehow, but refused to allow it to show. She said slowly, 'Thank you. But I don't feel particularly strong or calm inside. I just don't think it helps to let it show, you see. But when I'm absolutely sure Sarah's out of danger, I'll probably cry a bucket.'

She smiled tremulously at him and didn't resist as he tightened his grip on her hand. They sat like that in silence for what seemed a small eternity.

Then the swing doors opened wide and a figure moved through them, untying his mask at the same time, and Miranda felt as if her hand would break in the grip that held it in the instant before Nick stood up and exclaimed, 'David! Thank heavens you're here! How is she?'

'She's going to be all right, Nick.'

Miranda massaged her crushed fingers but found she had not the strength to stand up. She listened to the two men talking.

'I promise you, Nick, she's in no danger now, although it was lucky someone found her when they did.'

'It was Miranda here,' she heard Nick say. 'If it hadn't been for her . . .'

'I didn't do much,' Miranda heard herself interrupt from what seemed like a long way off as she felt tears run down her face and realised they were both looking at her with some concern. 'I'm all right,' she said weakly. 'At least I will be in a minute.'

The doctor said, 'I think it would be an idea if you both went home now. Sarah's under heavy sedation, so there's no more you can do for her.'

'I don't want to leave,' Nick said stubbornly. 'I want to be with her.'

'Nick, they'll let you look in on her now, but it will be a long time until she comes round. At least go home and freshen up. You'll feel better able to cope with this if you do. In the meantime I'm going to stay around and keep an eye on her. Trust me.'

Nick looked down at the stains on his shirt and then across at Miranda. 'You're right,' he said at last. 'She wouldn't want to see me like this anyway. Come on, Miranda.'

'This . . . isn't the way home,' Miranda said as her employer drove slowly and carefully through the deserted dark streets as if every movement was an effort for him.

He looked blankly across at her and Miranda bit her lip.

'It doesn't matter,' she said quietly. 'I can finish cleaning up. I don't think I would have been able to sleep . . .'

But the apartment was as clean and tidy as if there'd never been a party, they found when they arrived back. And there was a note from Samantha Seymour which Nick read with a twist of his lips and then tossed to Miranda as he strode across the room to pour a drink.

It read—Just gone home to change, Nick. I'll be back as soon as I can.

Miranda sat down on the wooden monk's chair and heard him dialling and then talking abruptly into the phone.

'She's going to be all right, Samantha . . . No, there's no point in your coming back here, because I won't be here. I want to be with her when she comes round . . . Yes, I appreciate that, you did well. Look, I'll be in touch.'

Miranda heard the receiver being set down sharply. She glanced up as he came over and handed her a drink and sat in the window seat. And was struck by how grim he looked.

'You shouldn't be angry with her,' she said tentatively. 'A lot of people can't stand the sight of blood.'

Nick stared down at the glass in his hand and she noticed how his eyelashes cast a shadow on his cheek.

'I don't suppose anyone else likes it either,' he said after a moment, and swirled the liquid in his glass. 'But you're right. Actually, I wasn't thinking about that so much as the fact that it was Samantha's idea to hold this party. She said Sarah would take it as a token of our affection for her. She couldn't have misread what Sarah needed more, though.' He looked up suddenly. 'I got the impression you didn't like her, anyway. Why should you try to defend her?' he asked abruptly.

Miranda opened and closed her mouth and bit her

lip ruefully. 'I don't think I ought to get into that,' she said finally. 'I really don't know her.' She shrugged and concentrated on her drink, and was surprised to hear him chuckle suddenly.

Her lashes flew up in surprise. 'What are you laughing at?' she asked uncertainly.

'You.'

'Why me?'

'Because it seems our Miranda from Beyond the Black Stump is learning some diplomacy,' he said with a grin that made her heart beat a strange tattoo. 'But you can say what you like about Samantha to me,' he added. 'Her talent for looking beautiful, and . . . certain other talents she has,' he narrowed his eyes, 'haven't ever blinded me to her faults.'

'I can just imagine what those other talents are,' Miranda retorted acidly as her so-called newly acquired diplomacy took wings, in a manner of speaking. 'Don't men ever think of anything else?' she demanded.

'Often,' he said idly. 'But not, generally, when it comes to beautiful women. For example,' he went on, and looked at her with an ironic quirk to his well-cut lips, 'for a few weeks back there I was rather . . . tormented by the shape of your breasts. And I found myself thinking of them in some unlikely places.'

Miranda, who had been in the act of sipping her whisky, gasped and choked, and was then subjected to the ignominy of seeing him smile lazily at her discomfort.

'You're surprised,' he said with that old glinting look of mockery back in his eyes when she was finally restored to equanimity. 'I didn't think you were that naïve.'

'I'm not, normally,' she said crossly, 'although— well, I suppose I am in a way, because . . .' She shrugged helplessly.

'You don't believe men think that way?'

'No! I mean, not all men all the time.' She moved uncomfortably, wanting to explain herself better but finding it almost impossible.

Nick laughed openly at her then. 'My dear Miranda,' he said at last, 'despite what you'd like to think, I bet there was not one man in that courtroom the day you were there, from the magistrate down to the doorman, who didn't undress you mentally. It isn't only a preoccupation of boundary riders and jumped-up jackeroos, believe me, if *that's* what you thought.'

He studied her hot face and downcast eyes cynically as she gritted her teeth in annoyance. But before she could reply suitably he went on, 'Don't tell me, though, it's only men who suffer from this aberration? Haven't you ever looked at a man and been attracted on a purely physical level? Before you got to know him, wondered what it would be like to touch him and have him touch you? Or do you make it a rule to get to know them thoroughly first—you know, talk for six weeks, hold hands for the next six, etc., etc., before you allow yourself those thoughts?'

Miranda contemplated her drink and wondered if he knew what he was doing to her. She wondered if he was doing it deliberately, if he'd somehow read her mind that day in court. Her hand shook slightly as she remembered the day in the shower with painful clarity, and a flash of anger mingled with hurt came to her heart.

'I don't know how we got on to this,' she said huskily, 'but since we have—yes, I suppose we all feel like it. What I object to, though, is just being considered a body. Like you and that awful police prosecutor did that day,' she said baldly. 'I don't think women separate bodies from personalities quite so . . .

coldbloodedly. If you must know, I think women are more realistic about it all.'

'Go on,' he drawled as she hesitated. 'I'm interested.'

She moved restlessly and then took a deep breath. 'Well, they don't tie their men to such a rigid set of statistics, for a start,' she said quietly. 'And I don't think they're so attracted by physique alone. I mean, if a man is a sensitive, intelligent lover they can live happily with the fact that he doesn't look like Robert Redford.'

She looked up to find him staring at her searchingly.

But he said unhurriedly, 'And how does Bill Hartley fit into your image of a sensitive, intelligent lover?'

'Very well,' she said quietly, 'for all he has a broken nose and I don't suppose his best friend would call him handsome exactly. But it's there all the same, something in his eyes ... and his hands, as every woman and girl for miles around could tell you,' she added wryly.

She paused and looked away as a sudden, unmistakable spark of speculation leapt into Nick's eyes. I bet he's wondering if I told the truth about not sleeping with Bill—or anyone, for that matter, she thought intuitively, and felt that flicker of anger grow.

'But for someone like yourself, say,' she went on without thinking too clearly, 'and so many men, it seems to be only the outward image that counts for most—it seems to me, anyway. Take that day in court. You decided you could 'put me down to experience', although you honestly—so you *said* anyway—believed I was an upcountry twit who'd tried to seduce the magistrate.' She shrugged as his eyes narrowed and glinted. 'And take Samantha Seymour. She might be very talented in bed and she's certainly one of the most beautiful women I've seen, but she's also the rightest snob I've ever met, and if you ask me, I don't think she's a very caring sort of person. But perhaps you could tell me differently?'

She looked at him enquiringly with the light of battle clearly in her eyes.

'No,' he said consideringly. 'But before that, I can't quite work out what annoyed you more that day. Was it that I said you weren't my type or, as you claim, that I said it but was still prepared to put to "put you down to experience"?'

Miranda's eyes were very bright and green as she said, 'If you want me to answer honestly—everything you said about me that day annoyed me. Are you trying to change the subject?' she added gently.

He grinned then, almost appreciatively. 'No, I don't think she's the most caring person in the world. But then I haven't really asked her for a commitment . . .'

'Well, maybe you should,' she interrupted. 'Or try it with someone else. It could do you the world of good, and then you might understand what I'm trying to say.'

'Are you offering yourself for the position?' he asked with another grin and quizzically raised eyebrows.

Miranda counted to ten beneath her breath and forced herself to relax. 'I'm sorry,' she said quietly. 'I didn't mean to lecture you. Why don't you go and get cleaned up? I haven't got anything to change into, so perhaps you could drop me off home on your way back to the hospital.' She looked around. 'There's nothing more I can do here.'

She watched the sombreness come back into his eyes until he looked away and she saw his shoulders slump slightly. 'Can you imagine how alone she must have felt to do something like that?' he said tautly. 'And I don't know how to help her,' he added almost inaudibly.

He stood up then and tossed off the rest of his drink. 'Miranda,' he said abruptly, 'spend the rest of the night here. After I've seen Sarah and taken some medical advice, I'd like to talk to you. You could borrow one of my pyjama tops or something, and you look exhausted anyway.'

'Well, I . . .'

'I won't be here until morning, if that's what you're worrying about,' he said with a tinge of impatience.

'It's not that . . .'

'What is it, then? Wouldn't you rather have a warm bath and crawl straight into one of the spare beds now? And if anything . . . unexpected should happen at the hospital, at least I can reach you on the phone here without disturbing anyone else.'

'All—all right, I'll stay,' she said, and found herself unexpectedly touched. 'Would you like me to come back to the hospital with you, though?'

Nick touched her cheek. 'You're really out on your feet, you know. Better get to bed, we wouldn't want two casualties. But thanks . . . for everything, friend.'

He turned away, shrugging off his jacket, and disappeared into his bedroom, and some minutes later the shower gushed.

But Miranda stayed where she was with her hand on her cheek, too shaken to move.

If he asked me now, she thought—well, I'd consent to anything he asked of me now. I'd do anything to comfort him to take away the tension and strain. She bit her lip.

CHAPTER SEVEN

MIRANDA awoke with the sunlight on her face and the sound of the doorbell in her ears. It took a minute or two to work out where she was, and then she pushed her hands sleepily through her hair and slipped out of bed. She looked around absently for a robe as the bell rang more stridently, but there wasn't one, and she looked helplessly down at herself, clad in a man's exotic jade-green silk nightshirt. She had found it in Nick's drawer and decided it would cover more of her than one of his pyjama tops. It had struck her at the same time that it was still brand new and never worn, and she had decided it was probably a present from someone with a raffish sense of humour, little realising how soon she was to discover her error.

'All right,' she muttered as the bell rang again, 'I'm coming!' and gave up her rather vague search for something to add to her attire. Perhaps it's him . . . he must have forgotten his keys, she thought, and hastened through to the vestibule.

But as she opened the door it was to see Samantha Seymour on the doorstep with her arm raised to attack the bell once more, and they both froze in surprise as they stared at each other.

'Oh,' Miranda spoke first to break the silence, 'it's you. Come in. He's not here, he's . . .'

Samantha dropped her arm and interrupted her. 'What the hell are you doing here?' she demanded. 'No, don't tell me,' she went on, not giving Miranda a chance to speak, 'I knew the minute I laid eyes on you that you were only after one thing. Well, it seems you've got your heart's desire, you cheap little whore!' Her voice roice shrilly.

'Hang on,' Miranda said dazedly. 'You're . . .'

'Don't tell me to hang on!' Samantha spat at her, and with a lightning move raised her arm again and slapped Miranda across the face. 'You have the most colossal nerve,' she went in a deadly undertone as Miranda staggered backwards. 'You're even wearing the nightshirt I gave him for his birthday. You must have bewitched him temporarily, but don't think you could ever hold him, Miranda, and shall I tell you why?' she offered as she stepped over the threshold and slammed the door shut behind her.

'I probably couldn't stop you,' Miranda murmured dazedly with her hand to her head, 'but there's no need, honestly . . .'

'Yes, there is,' Samantha snapped through her teeth, and shot Miranda a gaze that was white-hot with anger and emotion. 'Do you know what he really, honestly, thinks of you? He thinks you're a little country bumpkin, perhaps a bit brighter than most, but still destined to end up on a dirt farm with ten children, because that's about the sum total of you, Miranda, bedding and breeding!'

Miranda went pale. 'D-did he say that?' she asked in a voice that sounded unlike her own.

Samantha smiled unpleasantly. 'He said more, my dear. Why, only last night before . . . but there, I don't want to cause you any further distress.' She looked Miranda up and down. 'If I were you,' she went on more quietly, 'I'd run for my life. Because you could never have him, not even after what you did for Sarah last night. I know Nick, you see, and once he gets over this temporary lust for you,' she emphasised the word lust cruelly, 'he'll leave you with a broken heart. The

Nicholas Barretts of this world aren't for you, my dear. You've set your sights way too high. Go home, Miranda, and marry your bush cavalier, Bill Hartley. Take my advice if you have any scrap of sense!'

Miranda let her hand drop to her side. The mention of Bill's name seemed to add a ring of authenticity to Samantha's words. But did I doubt them? she wondered, and found she was shaking inwardly at the thought of the two of them discussing her and Bill and laughing gently. He had probably told her about Shirley Tate too . . .

Oh, I could die, she thought, and had to stop herself from breaking out into a wild frenzy and beating her fists against the wall. How could he do this to me?

A movement from Samantha brought her out of her reverie with a start, but only to stare at the other girl as if she had never seen her before, until a curiously puzzled expression crossed Samantha's beautiful features.

'Miranda?' she said just a shade uncertainly.

Miranda unclamped her lips. 'As it happens your advice was a little premature,' she said huskily, 'and I suspect not entirely unmotivated. But for what it's worth I'll take it. In fact you could pass on the message for me. Tell him I'm going home. You'll find him at the hospital, by the way. He's been there all night.'

She re-opened the front door.

Samantha hesitated. 'Miranda, I'm sorry I hit you.'

'I'll live,' Miranda said briefly.

'Seeing you in that nightshirt sort of . . . got to me,' Samantha went on uneasily.

'I guess it would,' said Miranda, unaware of how pale she still looked. 'But I had no idea how significant it was.' She hesitated herself as she surveyed the other girl. 'Miss Seymour, if you feel so strongly about him,' she said in a gentler voice, 'I think you should let him know and perhaps stand back. Otherwise it might be you nursing a broken heart.'

'. . . I don't know what you mean,' Samantha got out at last.

Miranda shrugged and thought briefly of repeating Nicholas's sentiments on the subject of Samantha Seymour, but she bit her tongue. Tit for tat isn't going to help me, she thought.

'Don't worry about it,' she said evenly. 'Look, are you going or staying?'

'Going,' said Samantha as she drew an invisible cloak of dignity about her. 'I think you're being very wise, Miranda, and I hope to God I never meet you again,' she added maliciously, her small moment of remorse forgotten.

'Me too,' Miranda muttered as she closed the door behind her and leant back against it. She tilted her head and stroked her throat distractedly as she felt the tears slide down her cheeks. 'But wasn't she right?' she admitted painfully. 'How can I stay? After hearing that and the way I *feel*. But how can I feel this way about someone I detest sometimes? And how to go home . . . feeling this way? And yet of all the people in the world, I need you now, Bill,' she sighed anguishedly as the tears fell thickly.

It was several minutes before she found the strength to push herself away from the doorway, and then it was to move to the phone in the study.

'I'm enquiring about Sarah Barrett,' she said after dialling and being switched through several nursing stations.

'Are you family?' a businesslike voice enquired.

'No,' Miranda replied wearily, 'but I was with her when she was admitted.'

'Ah yes,' the disembodied voice said, sounding suddenly enlightened. 'Her condition is stable, she's in no danger. Her brother is with her now. Would you like to speak to him?'

'No, thank you,' Miranda said hastily, 'if you're sure?'

'Quite sure,' the voice said firmly.

Miranda put the phone down slowly and stood staring out of the study window. The sparkling waters of the river reflected the early sunlight, but she didn't notice this. And it was with bleak eyes that she turned and surveyed the study and thought painfully of Nicholas Barrett.

She pictured him telling Samantha about her and wondered if he had mentioned catching her in the shower with the cooking sherry—wondered if that little story wasn't right now doing the rounds of Brisbane high society, thanks to Samantha. Then she thought of how close she had come just last night to throwing all her good intentions over the moon, how hard it was when she was with him not to succumb to the dictates of her treacherous body.

She scanned the bookshelves desolately and shivered suddenly. Oh yes, she thought, Samantha's right, I have only one choice, and that's to go. She shivered suddenly as the realisation hit her that this was the end to all her dreams of financial independence too. Her dreams of building up a catering business, because without Nick and the entrée he could give her it would be virtually impossible to get started, not to mention the fact that Samantha would probably find a way of undermining her anyway. And as she realised it, she understood fully for the first time just how much that particular dream had been sustaining her through the turmoil she had experienced since she had met Nick Barrett.

'Oh, Miranda,' she groaned, 'how did you get yourself into such a mess?'

I'm really right back where I started, she thought miserably. With an unfinished secretarial course which I've been neglecting lately because I've been living in some sort of a stupid dream world—and only one job that I hate anyway and isn't sufficient to do more than live off from day to day.

She grimaced as she thought of the meagre amount in her savings account. Of course there was still an unopened pay packet in her purse that she had received from Nick yesterday, but although she knew she would have been well recompensed for the party, even that wouldn't last longer than a few weeks if she didn't manage to get another job.

She sank down wearily behind the desk again and a sudden thought crystallised in her brain. She stared longingly at the phone and pictured how uncomfortably public the telephone at her lodgings was. And how difficult it was to have a private conversation from a phone booth.

Her heart beat uncomfortably, but suddenly the need to talk was too great and she was saying into the receiver, 'I'd like to put a call through to Goondiwindi, please.' She knew the number by heart. 'And when I'm finished, could you ring me back and tell me how much it is?' She put the receiver down and sat waiting tensely, praying that Nick wouldn't come home or try to ring her, although she was sure he wouldn't be leaving Sarah for some time.

The phone shrilled. She picked it up and said eagerly, 'Hello?'

'Miranda? Is that you?'

'Oh, Bill! How did you know?' she asked, smiling and brushing away the tears at the same time.

His deep, resonant voice came back to her down the line. 'I'd always know your voice, Miranda. How are you, petal?'

She caught her breath as she remembered his private name for her. 'I'm . . . not too sure. I . . . Bill? How are you?'

There was a momentary silence. Then he said very quietly, 'Missing you like hell, Miranda. Why are you crying, petal?'

'Because I'm missing you too, Bill,' she said through her tears. 'In fact I feel so homesick right now . . .' She sniffed and laughed weakly.

'Why don't you come home, then, my love?' The words sounded as if they were spoken with an effort and it hurt her almost unbearably to think of what he might be hoping she was going to say. She found she could picture him almost as if he was standing next her. His powerful body, probably no v clad in his khaki work clothes, his wide-brimmed hat close at hand, his big hands that could be so gentle too. The patient Border collie waiting for his master . . .

'Oh, Bill,' she said helplessly, 'I think I'm still as mixed up as I ever was only—maybe more so.'

He said nothing for a long moment. Then, 'Miranda, listen to me. For so long as it takes you to make up your mind, I'll be here. If you come home to me now I . . . well, if you're wondering whether I still love you, still want you, that's like asking me if I'm still breathing. But if you're not sure, I can wait.'

'Bill, you've waited so patiently for so long, how can I . . .'

His voice cut across hers, 'That's my affair, petal.' He sounded wry. He added gently, 'And that's the last reason you should pick for coming to me, Miranda. That's the one way I shouldn't want you. Miranda?'

'Yes, I'm still here, Bill,' she said huskily. 'I don't know how to thank you. Bill . . .' She closed her eyes and put into words, a shadowy, half-formulated plan that had been on the edge of her mind since Samantha's

visit. 'I'm leaving Brisbane, Bill. No,' she said quickly,
'you mustn't worry about me. I'm only going to take a
little holiday and try to sort myself out. I won't be
going far and I'll let you know where I am as soon as I
can.'

She thought she heard what sounded like a sigh come
down the line and winced, but all he said was, 'Promise
me that, petal. Because if I don't get a line or something from you in a day or two, I'll come down and
look for you. I . . . like just to know where you are.
And if you ever need me . . .'

'I promise, Bill,' she whispered into the phone.
'Goodbye.'

It was the shrilling of the phone again beneath her
hand that brought her out of her tearful reverie. She
picked it up again with her heart beating faster, but it
was only the exchange with the cost of the call. She
knew then there was only one thing left to do—to leave.
She stood up and looked round the study, wondering
bleakly why it was that nothing, not Samantha's cruel
words, not Bill, not even the sure knowledge that she
meant nothing to Nicholas Barrett, nothing made it
any easier to go. To take the step that would lock him
out of her life for ever.

Yet it's the only thing to do, Miranda, she told herself bitterly as she put on her bloodstained dress and
covered it with her pinafore. She left some money in
the kitchen to cover the phone call and flinched as she
thought of Nick finding it and wondering what it was
for. Just to think of him doing something as mundane
as pocketing some money filled her with the most curious flood of pain and anger and bitterness. But it was
that bitterness, in the end, that helped her to leave.

Hold on to it, Miranda, she urged herself throughout
the rest of that long day during which she made all the
arrangements to leave town. Hold fast, she thought

again as she was finally on the last coach heading for
the coast.

And the very next day she was lying on the beautiful
beach at Burleigh Heads admiring the Norfolk pines
and soaking up the Gold Coast sunshine with a
deliberately blank mind. She had hired an on-site
caravan at an adjacent caravan park for a week, which
was the cheapest way she knew of living, short of
camping, and which meant she could cook her own
meals—also a saving. It had pleased her in fact to find
that the caravan was cheaper than her lodgings in
Brisbane, particularly as she had to forgo a week's rent
there in lieu of notice.

The two cards she had sent that morning, one to
Bill and one to her family, were the only break she had
allowed in the rigid control she was keeping on her
thoughts and emotions; and she had stood before the
postbox for an age with Bill's card in her hand staring
down at the simple, friendly message just telling him
where she was and that she was all right, before posting
it.

But that night, in the cramped confines of the little
caravan with the sound of the surf in her ears, she
knew suddenly that she couldn't hide the truth any
longer. The true mainspring of the bitterness and the
pain she felt. The awful irony that if she had never
met Nicholas Barrett, she could have married Bill
and shared his country life with him and been
happy.

She wept then, in the dark, for Bill and for herself
because she now knew what it must be like for him.
But for the man who had done this to her, made it
impossible for her to think of loving anyone else, she
built up those barriers of bitterness again in her mind,
and made a vow to keep them up.

The weather was perfect for the next few days. Miranda swam in the surf, sunbathed, fished off the rocks with a hand-line and went for long moonlight walks. And she found herself almost unconsciously relaxing, although she was still rejecting all but the most necessary human contact. Even with the friendly families in the vans on either side of hers, not to mention the admiring looks and whistles that came her way on the beach. A few bolder men had tried to strike up an acquaintanceship with her, but she had looked so blank they had desisted.

By the end of the week, she glowed with health and vitality and knew she could no longer put off thinking of the future. So she scanned the local newspaper and after careful consideration decided that she could probably get a job as a waitress or a barmaid in this area that teemed with restaurants, if nothing else, so she booked the van for another week and resolutely crushed the thought that if she didn't get a job within a week, she would have no choice but to go home. Home and Bill. The thought made her close her eyes in pain. How could she inflict that torture on Bill . . .

She was still thinking of this the next morning when she literally bumped into Nick in the busy shopping centre of Burleigh Heads just as she was about to go into the supermarket.

For a second she couldn't believe her eyes. She had been fishing and the breeze had whipped her hair into a tangle of streaky fairness. The blouse she wore over her costume was still damp with sea-spray and her long, bare legs were beautifully brown and shoeless.

'You!' she exclaimed incredulously as she stared up into his hard, dark eyes and felt his fingers bite into her upper arm. 'What are you doing here?'

He looked her up and down silently for a long, tense moment. Then he said very coolly, 'Coincidentally, the same as you, it seems, Miranda. I'm taking a few days off.'

'Who's looking after Sarah?' she asked involuntarily.

He narrowed his eyes. 'Now I wonder why you would care about that, Miranda,' he said softly but with an edge of contempt that cut through her. 'Forgive me if I was wrong,' he went on unevenly, 'but I thought you'd washed your hands of Sarah. Not that she had any claim on you, of course ...'

'It wasn't like that,' Miranda interrupted in a trembling voice. 'I care very much about what happens to Sarah, but ... well, it's difficult to explain,' she said raggedly, and wondered what unkind twist of fate had sent her stumbling into this nightmare.

Nick raised his eyebrows ironically. 'I can imagine,' he said curtly. 'It's just that I find it a little difficult to fit in with your sermonising on the subject of ... caring.' He dropped his hand and shrugged. 'But as I said before, she had no claim on you.'

'But you *don't* understand!' Miranda said hotly, and then looked around selfconsciously as she realised her raised voice had created a ripple of interest amongst the passers-by.

'Well, if you think you can enlighten me, you're welcome to try. But I don't think this is quite the place,' he added dryly. 'My car is parked over there.' He turned her around with a hand on her shoulder and she stumbled and hesitated and then pulled back.

'I don't want to go anywhere with you,' she muttered.

'Because you're a coward, my dear,' he said through his teeth as that dark, mocking glance raked her mercilessly from head to foot. 'In fact you're worse. You're the kind of person who goes around moralising on top of it. Look,' he grated, 'you might enjoy making a spectacle of yourelf, in fact you seem to have a particular talent for it, but I don't. If you're going to come, come quietly. If not you can go to hell.'

Miranda licked her lips. 'Well, I may be a lot of things,' she said in a fierce undertone, 'in fact *you've* had a lot of fun calling me a lot of things, but if you think I'm afraid of you, you're quite mistaken. It'll give me a great deal of pleasure to tell you a few home truths. Right, folks!' she turned to the small knot of interested spectators and waved at them. 'The show's over,' she said brightly through her rage. 'This way, my dear Mr Barrett,' she added over her shoulder. 'I see your car now . . .'

And she stalked off in the most magnificent rage she could ever recall experiencing.

It stayed with her too as he unlocked the door for her. Stayed with her as they drove up the headland to an imposing block of units and intensified as she realised he was laughing quietly at her.

'I hate you,' she said coldly and clearly as he nosed the car into an underground parking area. 'I hate you and despise you more than I've ever hated anyone!'

'Do you,' he said with a faint grin that took her right back to the first time she had seen him in the court-room. 'I must admit that whatever else I think about you Miranda, you're never dull to be with. I've changed my mind about you, in fact. I don't think cooking is your métier at all.' He switched the car off and turned to her. 'You could be a one-woman circus most successfully—indeed magnificently.'

It had happened to her before and it should have warned her, but it didn't. She lunged at him like a wildcat, her green eyes ablaze with fury. But he fielded the attack effortlessly and she ended up in his arms, her body twisted across his lap and her heart beating violently in the moment before he lowered his dark head because she knew in that instant the punishment she had so thoughtlessly invited.

It was a savage, merciless kiss, and she could never afterwards put her finger on the moment when her efforts to escape changed to something very different. It could have been when she managed to get her hands free only to find that instead of wanting to tear at his hair she only wanted to run her fingers through it lingeringly. Or maybe it was what his own hands were doing to her body, she wondered briefly at the time, as he ran his fingers down her spine and then up again to push her swimsuit strap from one shoulder and just lightly slide two fingers about her exposed nipple.

But whenever it was, when the kiss ended she lay shuddering in his arms and wondered at the curious feeling at the pit of her stomach, her rage and fury forgotten.

'This is what it's all about, isn't it, Miranda?' said Nick, speaking very softly as his eyes roamed her face in his arms. 'This is why you ran away. You couldn't face this, could you?'

She didn't answer, found she couldn't and had to clench her fists to stop her hands from wandering over his shoulders beneath his shirt. I've wanted to do that for so long, she thought mindlessly.

He sat her up then and surveyed her unsmilingly. 'Do you think we could go in now and . . . talk turkey, as the Yanks say? Or are you going to play the outraged virgin on me? You're quite free to, you know. All you have to do is open that door.' He looked pointedly at the doorhandle beside her.

Miranda closed her eyes and knew she was in no state to be running anywhere. So what do I do now? she thought. I can't even think straight.

But she made what seemed like an incredible effort. 'Nick,' she said huskily, 'I can't do it. When I'm away from you I know that in all sanity.'

'And when you're kissing me?' he asked with a curious sombreness.

Her head drooped so that he couldn't see the bleakness that came to her eyes. 'All the good sense I ever had warns me to distrust . . . how you made me feel just now.'

He said into the small silence, 'What if we changed the terms, broadened the scope of this . . . conflict?'

She tensed and looked at him obliquely from beneath her lashes not sure what he meant and suddenly frightened. Because in the close confines of his car, even in the dimness, he seemed to be so big and his cream linen trousers and dark shirt only served to highlight the breadth of his shoulders and the latent strength of his thighs.

'If you mean . . . we go to bed,' she said hesitantly, 'I . . .'

'I meant if we got married,' he said dryly, and smiled faintly at her stunned face.

Miranda set her glass down carefully on a wrought iron table beside her and looked around dazedly. She was seated on a wide, shaded balcony that led out from the lounge of the unit and seemed to be almost suspended above the sparkling waters of the bay beneath.

Nick sat down opposite her in a cane lounger and regarded her thoughtfully over the rim of his glass. She looked away and spoke for the first time since he had led her from the car, and said the first thing that came to mind, 'Are you renting this for your holiday?'

He lifted one eyebrow. 'The family owns it.'

'It's very nice,' she replied after a moment, and thought how strange life was. I had to pick the one beach on the whole of the Gold Coast where the family owns a unit . . .

'Yes, it is,' he agreed politely. 'Would you like a guided tour through it?'

'No, thank you,' she said hastily, and coloured at the fleeting look of amusement in his eyes. 'Well, what am I supposed to say?' she asked tightly.

'Yes or no is the generally accepted form for dealing with proposals of marriage, I guess,' he drawled. 'Try your drink,' he advised. 'You'll find it very refreshing.'

Miranda bit her lip and said at last, her voice very low, 'You can't seriously expect me to believe you want to marry me?'

'But I do.'

She stared at him. '*Why?*' she whispered.

Nick looked at her meditatively. 'I was surprised once before at how naïve you can be, Miranda. I suppose I could say because it's the only way I could get you to go to bed with me.'

'Well, don't!' she warned fiercely, her eyes suddenly flashing green fire.

'I wasn't planning to. Besides, it wouldn't be quite true, would it?' He looked at her faintly derisively. 'If you think back to how you felt down there in the car, in the apartment and on a certain day—a day which more or less precipitated this, when you omitted to lock a certain bathroom door . . .'

'You make it sound as if I did that deliberately,' she interrupted with a catch in her voice. 'I wasn't expecting you home for another two hours.'

'I know,' he said evenly. 'I'm not accusing you of inviting it. But it's getting harder each time, isn't it? For both of us.' He said the words flatly.

'It,' she hesitated, 'wouldn't be so hard if you just let me go.'

'That's debatable,' he said. 'And this is another option, isn't it? Look, despite what I've just said, Miranda, I can't deny it's a rather basic feeling that motivates me. But then I never did try to deny it.'

'I don't understand,' she said confusedly.

'Dear Miranda,' he said, smiling crookedly, 'don't you understand that whatever it is between us, it's a very powerful thing? If it wasn't, would you be here now?'

She leant her head back and tried to think. Would she?

'Motivation,' she said at last. 'I don't know why, but that's another thing I distrust.'

'Put it this way, then, if the word disturbs you. We're quite alone here now. No one could interrupt us. We could finish our drinks, like this.' He drained his glass and went on very quietly, 'Then I could reach out a hand to you like this.'

Miranda stared at his hand as it lay on her own just lightly.

'And I could take you by the hand, Miranda,' he said even more quietly, 'and lead you to the bedroom and undress you very slowly so that I could savour every inch of your beautiful body, delicately, slide my hands from your shoulders to your toes, taste the salt on you from the sea. Worship you with my hands and my mouth until you begged me to take you . . .'

Oh Heavens! she thought as the skin on the inside of her wrist broke into a fine trembling that she couldn't control or restrain from spreading up her arm, please help me.

'None . . . none of this,' she stammered raggedly, 'really explains why you want to marry me.'

Nick sat back then and removed his hand, looking at her with a sudden detachment that came like a blow in the face.

'Much as it might surprise you, I do have some ethics, my dear,' he said coolly. 'It may be only sex we want from each other, but at least if I'm going to lead a . . . lead someone like you to it, I can give you something in return.'

'What?' Miranda whispered. 'A divorce?'

He shrugged. 'Who knows? We might surprise ourselves.'

She stared at him, searching for a note of cynicism that would belie his words, and was suddenly shaken because she could find none. He was looking at her as levelly as he had spoken. She tried to speak, but found she couldn't.

Then the moment was past and he said with his old, enigmatic look, 'You must admit, though, you'd be better off being the former Mrs Nicholas Barrett than just plain Miranda Smith—second-hand but well run in.'

She shivered at her own well-remembered phrase and closed her eyes, trying desperately to concentrate. Would I? she thought. Or would I be in more desperate straits than ever? Isn't it time you got right to the kernel, Miranda? You thought you'd stripped off all the layers—you worked out that it was because of him you couldn't go to Bill; and you allowed the bitterness you felt to cloud the fact that you couldn't put this man out of your heart because despite everything, you *love* him, and the thought of living without him, even just to see and speak to is . . . unbearable. That being in love with someone doesn't change if that love isn't returned. It's still there whatever. Yet isn't that all the more reason to start trying to live without him *now*?

She opened her eyes and licked her lips. She started to speak, but he interrupted her abruptly, 'There's something else, Miranda. Two things.'

She looked bemused.

'There's the question of money,' he said straightly.

Miranda flushed and an angry spark leapt to her eyes. 'I'd never marry for money,' she said tautly.

'Oddly enough I believe you,' he said, and looked amused. 'Yet I can't help but know ... how you're placed, as they delicately phrase it. Or your alternatives, which seem to me to be rather limited. Get some sort of a job down here, possibly little better than the one you had in Brisbane—or go home.' He watched her, his eyes narrowed and more than usually acute, she thought.

'I ...'

'No, hear me out first, Miranda.'

'If it's going to be as humiliating as your first point, don't bother,' she said in a tight little voice.

'I'm sorry. It's Sarah,' he said evenly. 'You're the one person I know who could help her out of this mess. You're the only person I can think of who could talk some sense into her because you have a basic, homespun philosophy about you and such a down to earth practicality besides being the most honest person I know that would help her far more than all the psychiatry in the world. I've spoken to several experts on the subject and they seem to agree.'

'But why do I have to marry you, to help Sarah?' she asked faintly.

'Because I'm taking Sarah to live with me. Not at the apartment but a house I inherited. It has a beautiful garden and a self-contained unit for her. But I don't think,' he said with some irony, 'that you and I could live under the same roof without some form of agreement between us. Do you?' His dark eyes held hers steadfastly.

Until she raised her hands to her face distractedly. 'I can't think straight,' she whispered. 'What would I do with my time—apart from Sarah?' She stopped abruptly and felt a chill of shock that she should even be considering the pros and cons.

'You could devote the rest of it to me,' he said with

a grin and a look from beneath his half-closed lids that sent the most incredible sensations through her. 'I should think we'll run hot for a fair while, whatever the final outcome.'

Miranda stumbled to her feet. 'I can't do it!' she said hoarsely. 'It just seems so cold-blooded!' and flinched as he laughed at her with his eyes, because she knew he was thinking of her anything but cold-blooded responses earlier in the car.

'Very well.' Nick stood up and shrugged too. 'I was right, wasn't I?' he said almost casually. 'You are a coward. You'd rather spend the rest of your life wondering about . . . us, wouldn't you?'

She took an unexpected breath that jolted her and knew that what he'd said was all too true. She would spend the rest of her life wondering. The thought shook her to the roots of her soul. Wondering if I could perform a miracle and make him love me? *Am* I a coward? To think that it's just not possible, not to want to take a chance? Who said it—about it being better to have loved and lost than never to have loved at all?

She lifted her head at last, the confusion and turmoil she felt etched plainly in her eyes.

They stared at each other for what seemed like a small eternity, Nick's dark eyes boring into her green ones. Then very slowly he put out his hand again, and after a moment Miranda lifted her own and put it in his.

He stared down at their joined hands and then lifted his eyes to hers. 'Is this a full capitulation, Miranda?'

'I don't know,' she said huskily. 'I . . .'

He touched her lips with his free hand. 'I understand. So be it,' he said on a curiously wry note but with an underlying gentleness. 'Come on.' He led her indoors.

It was just as he had said it would be.

He undressed her slowly as he had promised and laid her on cool emerald green sheets with her hair spread out in beautiful disarray, and just stood looking down at her for some minutes.

Miranda fought the sudden panic-stricken shyness that threatened to freeze her golden body to its emerald background and forced herself to hold his gaze steadfastly but with wide, wary eyes.

And a little later when he was on the bed beside her just stroking her from her breasts to her thighs he murmured, 'Why don't you try touching me?'

She responded slowly at first and in an agony of fear that she would seem hopelessly unskilled by comparison. But the feel of his broad smooth shoulders beneath her fingertips seemed to soothe her fears and she felt herelf relax gradually and let her hands wander over the long, strong lines of his back.

She felt a tiny flame begin to burn deep within her and the most beautiful feeling of sensuous languor come to her limbs beneath his roving hands. Until she moved against the sheets in an unconscious invitation and saw a faint gleam of admiration in his dark eyes just before he lowered his head to tease her nipples into full bloom with his tongue.

She heard herself moan with pleasure then and ran her fingers through his thick, dark hair, unable to control the shudders that racked her body at the exquisite pleasure he was inflicting on her. And the flame grew and grew just as he had predicted, although he hadn't mentioned the urgency she would feel to bring him the same ecstasy he was bringing her.

Perhaps it was the urgency, she thought later, that helped her not to falter when the delicacy of his embrce became more demanding. To welcome it, in fact, to move beneath him and gasp finally, 'Please . . . yes . . .!'

To welcome the pain and stifle the cry that rose to her throat as an inescapable part of it, although she couldn't hold back the tears that came.

Tears which Nick not long afterwards traced down her cheeks after they'd lain side by side breathing deeply.

He stared at her broodingly. 'I was wrong—you're not a coward. And you were a virgin. I compliment you.'

Miranda blinked and resisted an impulse to catch his hand and rest it on her lips. 'Did you really doubt it?' she murmured.

'I . . . wondered, shall we say,' he answered.

'Perhaps I should have worn a placard,' she managed to say unevenly. 'Another one.' She turned away and trembled as she thought of what she had really wanted to say. I love you . . .

'Perhaps you should have,' she heard him reply, and tensed as she felt his fingers trace the outline of her hip. 'Now will you marry me, Miranda?'

Shock held her rigid because all along a tiny part of her mind had refused to believe this. Then she turned back to him with wide eyes, to see him propped up on one arm staring at her intently.

'Because I was a virgin after all?' she whispered involuntarily.

Nick grimaced slightly. 'I didn't seriously doubt it,' he said after a moment. 'It's not something you can know, absolutely. But nothing else has changed, has it? Unless you were disappointed?'

Hasn't it? she thought, and trembled.

'You knew I wouldn't be, didn't you?' she said with a slight crack in her voice. 'I must seem very naïve to you,' she added with an effort.

'Naïve,' he agreed gravely, 'and very gallant.'

'Wasn't it any good for you?' she said before she

could stop the words, and bit her lip in embarrassment
as hot colour flooded her cheeks. He studied it and
then lifted a hand to trace the tide of it down her throat.

'It was very good for me, my dear,' he said finally as
if he could read the vulnerability in her eyes. 'If we
agree to disagree about most other things, I have to
admit I'm incredibly attracted to you. I watched just
about every emotion from plain fear to the most honest
giving I think I've ever known pass through your green
eyes while we made love.' He hesitated and then said
not quite evenly, 'Look, I know I'm not offering you
what your parents had. Despite your convictions, I
don't think it's in me to tell you I'll love you until
death us do part ... because I couldn't guarantee it.
But now, I want you and I need you. As I think you
want me, maybe need me.'

She felt herself smiling suddenly, although only she
knew it was the reverse side of tears.

'If there's one thing I admire about you, it's your
honesty,' she said slowly as she searched her soul and
recognised that, strangely, it was this quality—his
honesty—that was pushing her over the edge, giving
her the strength to take the chance.

'All right,' she said, 'I will marry you. If—' she
stopped, 'if you promise me one thing. Don't ever stop
being honest with me.'

She thought she imagined the suddenly bleak look
that came to his eyes, because it was gone before it
could take root, to be replaced by something else she
couldn't name.

But she forgot it as he slid an arm round her and
pushed a tendril of hair behind her ear. 'I could wax
poetical now in the best traditions, Miranda. Or I could
tell you jokes.' He dropped a light kiss on her hair.

'Why?' she whispered. 'I mean ...'

'Because I'd like to make you laugh,' he said

seriously but with a quirk to his lips.

She stared up at him bemused.

'Mmm,' he went on consideringly. 'Then when the tears are gone, we could do whatever you liked, provided we came back here and did this again fairly soon. Unless,' he tilted her face up to his, 'you'd rather stay here?'

Oh no, Miranda thought, how could I ever be able to forget him?

But she said with a catch in her voice, 'Some . . . poetry always did make me laugh.'

Nick's fingers moved beneath her chin. 'And then?'

She could see the smile lurking in his eyes and felt herself responding, couldn't help herself. She said demurely, 'It depends on the quality of your poetry, doesn't it?'

'Oh well, if that's the case,' he said teasingly, 'prepare yourself for a long siege.'

'Why, you . . .!' she protested, but he brought his lips down firmly on hers so that she could only shake with laughter that was still dangerously close to tears until he embraced her gently and her body stopped trembling beneath his hands.

'There,' he said into her hair. 'Feel better?'

She nodded wordlessly as he lifted his head and stared into her eyes.

'Would you like to try it again? It should be even better for you this time. But speaking relatively, we have all the time in the world.' He traced the outline of her lips. 'It's up to you.'

CHAPTER EIGHT

TIME, Miranda thought, and wished fervently she could get it out of her mind. I feel as if I'm living in a time machine. Or on the edge of a precipice.

She sat back on her heels and surveyed the plants about her. Then she pulled off her gardening glove and the diamond ring on her left hand caught the dappled sunlight and reflected it brilliantly in a burst of violet and rose fire.

After all, we've only been married for a month, she thought absently as she plucked a white daisy from the bush beside her and absently bit the stem. And only just moved into this beautiful old house with its fine view over the bay and gloriously tangled garden which attracted her like a magnet.

But instead of seeing Moreton Bay as she gazed out between the trees, the last month seemed to unfold before her eyes. The honeymoon they had taken before the wedding, just three golden days on the Coast from the day they had met so coincidentally in the main street of Burleigh Heads. Then the trip back to Brisbane and the quiet register office wedding with only Mrs Marshall and David Mackenzie, the doctor Nick had called to attend Sarah, as witnesses.

If Mrs Marshall had been surprised at her employer's precipitous marriage and his choice of bride, she had contained it admirably. Indeed, Miranda thought, she had even looked faintly smug afterwards as she had congratulated Nicholas and hugged Miranda warmly. But maybe I was imagining it, she thought, because if she was really happy for us, she was probably the only one. His older sister certainly wasn't . . .

She shivered slightly as she remembered being presented 'cold', as she thought of it to herself, to Lilian Seymour, whose existence she hadn't even been aware of until an hour or so earlier. Just as Lilian hadn't known of hers, and her eyes had bulged visibly when presented to her brother's bride, and her beautifully preserved face had looked suddenly old.

'Have you gone mad, Nick?' she had demanded. 'When did this happen? And who is she anyway?'

'My *wife*,' her brother had replied cuttingly. 'You may take it or leave it, Lilian. You don't have to speak your mind about it.'

But there had been worse to come. It had appeared that Lilian now considered herself responsible for Sarah, and she had reacted violently to Nick's plans for her.

'But . . . but,' she had spluttered foolishly, 'you can't do that! Sarah doesn't even know the girl! No, I won't hear of this, Nick. If you choose to go bush yourself, there's not much I can do about it,' she had added angrily, and Miranda knew then that Lilian had heard of her and placed her. 'But Sarah stays with me and Lawrence, and there's nothing *you* can do about *that*!'

'Oh, but there is, Lilian,' her brother had answered with deadly menace. 'And I will, if I have to have her certified mentally incompetent, which as her trustee I could do. It's about time she did get to meet the girl who saved her life, anyway.'

Miranda shivered slightly and picked another daisy.

Then there had been her own family's reaction to the news of her marriage. She had written two incredibly difficult letters to Goondiwindi the day after the wedding, not knowing what to expect in return.

She looked down at the daisy she was twisting in her hands and re-experienced the shock and surprise she had felt a few days later when she had opened the apartment door one evening . . .

'Dad! Oh, Dad . . .' She stared and then flung herself into his arms laughing and crying at the same time. 'Oh, Dad!'

'I had to come, Mirry,' he said gruffly, and stroked her hair as if she was still a little girl. 'I had to see for myself if you were happy.'

'Come in. Did you drive down? Oh, you must stay the night at least—I can't let you go so soon. Nick?'

But Nick was already standing behind them, his hand outstretched.

'Mr Smith,' he said courteously. 'It's a pleasure to meet you.'

Miranda was still hanging on to her father's arm, so she felt him tense slightly and held her breath, for in her heart of hearts she knew exactly what reservations he must have about her marrying a complete stranger in such a rush and in secret.

And she felt her own muscles tautening as he put out his hand after a perceptible hesitation and murmured, 'How do you do? I hope you don't mind me appearing out of the blue like this, but she's the only daughter I've got.'

Then a curious thing happened. The two men stared at each other, her father assessingly, critically and with a hint of the pain he felt showing clearly on his weathered, tanned face.

Nick didn't say anything, only accepted the look unflinchingly as if he knew and understood everything the older man was feeling and was acknowledging it.

Miranda watched and wondered fearfully at this unspoken communication. It was her father who broke the long tense moment. He seemed to relax slightly as if he had read something in Nick that had allayed his fears somewhat.

He twisted his broad-brimmed hat in his hands and said, 'Well, Mirry, if you were to offer me a cup of tea, I wouldn't say no.' He patted her cheek.

Miranda breathed again and flew to make him tea and a snack. She knew it wasn't all resolved, only the first hurdle cleared, but that was something. And as they sat and drank tea she couldn't prevent the happiness shining in her face. She was full of eager questions about home, and Nick, surprisingly—or not so surprisingly, she thought afterwards—discussed cattle and horses and the price of beef, so knowledgeably with her father that a glint of almost admiration came to his eyes.

They talked until nearly midnight and her father never mentioned the hasty, secret marriage, but she could tell that he was watching them both all the time, had still not quite dropped his guard.

Finally Nick stood up and said, 'I'll head for bed, I think. You two might like to have some time alone. Goodnight, sir. If you change your mind and decide you could take a couple more days off . . .?'

Her father stood up. 'Thanks, Nick, I appreciate it. But we're in the middle of a muster, that's why I have to leave at the crack of dawn tomorrow. But any time you'd like to come up home you'd be welcome. In fact, if you don't bring her up to see us often—well, we'll all just as likely descend on you, so be warned!'

He said it with a smile and again Miranda was aware of something flowing between her father and Nick that she wasn't privy to.

He turned to her as Nick left them. 'I hope you will,' he said gravely. 'We all miss you too much.'

'Dad?' she said questioningly as she took his hand.

'No, Miranda,' he said gently, 'you don't have to explain it to me. I do have faith in you. For one thing, you're so like your mother, for another I only have to look at you to see there's a sort of a glow about you. And there are some things between a man and a woman you can't explain to anyone. Only . . .' He hesitated.

'Don't you like him?' she asked after a moment.

'I do. He's a man—a man's man. But sometimes we men, in our ignorance—and I did it too—think women only fulfil one role. Your mother taught me different.' He looked at her searchingly, examining the faint colour that came to her cheeks, although her eyes didn't falter. He pressed her hand then lovingly and said gently, 'But there, I said before, you're the image of your mother. Just think on it when you need to, Mirry.'

Miranda sighed and came back to the present. She wasn't sure how her father had worked it all out, but she knew he had. She couldn't be sorry either because it seemed to lift the burden a little.

She thought of the note she had received from Bill not long after her father's visit—simple and warm sounding and written, she knew, in an effort to cut the invisible barrier that made going back to Goondiwindi so difficult . . . If you're happy, it makes me happy, Miranda, because you were the most beautiful thing I ever laid my eyes on . . .

'I wonder if I am happy,' she mused, still chewing absently on a daisy stalk. 'It's been a month now.'

She stared down at the diamond on her finger and tried to analyse just how it felt to be married to Nicholas Barrett, one of the youngest and most brilliant barristers in the state. It had been a busy month, with Nick going to work every day while she had organised the move from the apartment to this house and worked to get the old place in order. But in another sense it had been a quiet month. They hadn't entertained or been entertained and she had concentrated on trying to grow into his life style as well as she could, which had meant quite a lot of time on her own not only while he worked but when he brought work home, which he did frequently.

'And yet I don't think I've ever felt this intensely alive before,' she murmured to herself. She grimaced faintly. 'Or as much as if I was walking a tightrope and making war, not love!'

She closed her eyes and found that even after a month she still felt hot and shaken when she thought of them together in bed. Of how Nick could be savage and tender by turns, of how he treated her body like a personal possession and still insisted on undressing her himself before making love to her. And how his dark eyes glinted with something she couldn't name at her own growing confidence and how he was sometimes gentle and teasing, as he had been that first day, and encouraging, so that she felt all woman, alluring and infinitely desirable.

But at other times, when they were not in bed, it was a curious relationship, she thought. They got on well enough, so far at least, but there was an absence of something she couldn't quite put her finger on. Unless it was affection. Yes, she realised with a sudden quickening of her heart. For two people so close in one sense they were strangely aloof in another.

That's it, she thought. It's as if there's a little white line between us. Something that prevents me from, say, curling up in his lap just to talk or watch television. And then I feel as if he's . . . sort of sceptical about me, maybe testing me, but I don't know what for. It was like that after that awful interview with his sister Lilian. We didn't discuss it or even have a row about it, she thought with a faint quirk to her lips. I guess that's the difference between love and . . . lust?

She looked questioningly through the spreading

branches of a Giant Moreton Bay Fig for a long time and then nearly died of fright as she felt a hand on her shoulder and turned to look up into the dark, quizzical eyes of her husband.

'A daisy for your thoughts?' he said.

'Oh.' Miranda smiled and coloured faintly and removed the flower from her mouth. 'Nothing much. This garden fascinates me. I'd like to really work on it—if you don't mind.'

'Why should I?' he said after a moment, and helped her to her feet. 'Is that another of your talents, gardening?'

'I don't know,' she confessed. 'But I'd like it to be.'

'Well, good luck,' he said idly, and surprised her by picking another daisy and pushing it into her hair just above her ear. 'I didn't realise they were such a delicacy,' he said gravely. 'But they look very decorative too. I brought someone home with me, by the way—Sarah. She's unpacking now.'

Miranda was shocked when she met Sarah Barrett again. Shocked to see how thin and pale she was, and how tortured she looked and how uncertain.

So it was a tense, awkward moment, and Miranda's eyes flew to Nick's apprehensively because she was suddenly afraid that he'd coerced her into coming. Maybe Lilian had been right . . .

But Sarah ended the awkwardness herself by saying, 'Miranda, I haven't had a chance to thank you for what you did. I should have been shot for inflicting that on you—and Nick.'

'Don't worry about it,' Miranda said gruffly. 'I'm just so happy you've come to stay with us.' And she reached out and hugged the other girl naturally and unaffectedly, and a deep, deep resolve took root within her as she felt Sarah tremble. I'll make her better, if it's the last thing I do! she thought.

They had dinner together that night, although Sarah had a completely self-contained flatlet with its own private entrance on a side verandah.

'I shan't be doing this often, Nick,' she said with just a hint of her former liveliness in her great dark eyes as she picked at her food.

'You can do it as often as you like,' he replied easily. 'Miranda has this passion for cooking, and a third person would give her extra scope.'

'Miranda is also a very new bride,' Sarah said with a smile, and her first reference to her brother's marriage. 'I'm sure the last thing she wants is someone playing gooseberry, like Banquo's ghost. I'm sorry,' she said abruptly, and pushed her plate away. 'It's not your cooking, Miranda, I just don't seem to have any appetite. If you'll excuse me, I think I'll go to bed. Don't look at me like that, Nick,' she said tautly. 'I'm not going to do anything!' And she turned to run from the room as he half rose from his chair.

'Let her be, Nick,' Miranda said gently. 'It's going to take time.'

'It . . . it might not be as simple as Shirley Tate either,' he said grimly.

'I didn't ever think it would be. That won't stop me from trying, though.' She tilted her chin defiantly at him. 'Unless you're having second thoughts on the subject?'

She saw him relax suddenly. 'No, I'm not,' he said evenly. 'It's just . . . I hate to see her this way.'

'What are you doing, Miranda?' Sarah asked as she strolled round the wide verandah and came across Miranda tatting.

Miranda's heart quickened, for in the two weeks since Sarah's arrival this was the first sign of interest she had shown in any of her activities.

She explained about the tatting. 'My mother taught me,' she said with a grin. 'She claimed it was the best nerve-soother she knew.'

Sarah raised her eyebrows. 'I wouldn't have thought you needed soothing,' she remarked. 'If you have any deep traumas you hide them very well.'

'I'm not doing it for my nerves,' Miranda said lightly.

'Not for mine either, I hope,' said Sarah with narrowed eyes as she watched the shuttle fly in Miranda's fingers. 'I had enough occupational therapy of that nature while I was in hospital. And it was a whole lot easier than that looks,' she added dryly.

'It's not for my nerves or yours,' Miranda said with a chuckle. 'It's for the dining room table. The surface is so beautiful it seems a shame to hide it with a table-cloth, so I thought I'd make a set of place mats. Let's see, though,' she went on reminiscently, and rested her hands in her lap, 'I set out to make two doilies for two aunts of mine one Christmas. I think they got them three Christmases later.'

Sarah glanced at her. 'I'm surprised you haven't wanted to redecorate the whole place. All the furniture is rather old-fashioned, isn't it?'

'Is it?' Miranda said after a moment. 'I thought it was rather timeless and beautiful. But I must admit I'm no expert,' she added ruefully.

'Timeless is right,' Sarah said ruefully. 'In fact it forms part of my earliest recollections. I suppose Nick has told you this is our ancestral home? We all grew up here. The flatlet was created for our dear Grand-mamma and she bitterly resented being shut off from the family as she claimed. But then again she'd lived here all her married life, so I suppose it was hard for her to take a back seat. I suppose you also realise what a difficult family you've married into, Miranda? I sometimes think Nick is the only sane one among us.'

Too sane perhaps, Miranda felt like saying, but didn't.

'Well, I've only met two of his relatives so far,' she said.

Sarah interrupted and pulled a face. 'Lilian,' she said expressively. 'All I can say is thank God you married Nick and rescued me from Lilian's clutches, Miranda. You couldn't have any idea how timely it was. If I wasn't already insane, she was going to drive me to it. She kept *lecturing* me!'

Miranda smiled faintly and wondered if Sarah would ever know precisely how timely her brother's marriage had been. But she didn't waste too much time on that thought. Instead she took the first opening Sarah had so far presented her with. Not much of an opening, but at least a willingness to talk.

She said idly, 'Lilian didn't approve of me. I guess I can understand why.' She shrugged. 'Not that I really care—well, yes, I do. I can't help wishing I felt more the part. It's a bit of a jump from being his——, she hesitated, then said bluntly, 'his maid. Which a lot of people must know. Also, from the other side, so to speak, you're quite sure you know how to do things correctly, dress and so on, but it's a bit nerve-racking to enter a much more sophisticated society, which it is. I must say it bothers me sometimes,' she confessed, not without some candour.

But she trembled as Sarah surveyed her acutely and wondered if she would recognise it for the ploy it was—a bid to draw Sarah out of herself.

'Miranda!' Sarah exclaimed at last. 'You surprise me. I didn't think you worried about trivia like that.'

'Who doesn't?' Miranda said with a slight shrug.

'Isn't it only human?' she added quite genuinely.

'I ... guess it is,' Sarah agreed after a moment. 'What do you plan to do about it?'

Miranda grinned. 'Trial and painful error, probably.' She picked up her tatting and decided not to press it any more. She changed the subject. 'Who used to play the piano?'

'I did. I ...' Sarah stopped and bit her lip, but Miranda's ears had detected something, a different note in Sarah's voice that even the faint tinge of hopelessness couldn't drown.

She said, 'Piano's get to me. It's such a pure sound, isn't it? When you hear a piano concerto and the piano comes in clear and beautiful,' she shrugged. 'Sometimes it makes me shiver and break out into a sweat. It's my favourite instrument. And,' she grinned, 'it was like a blight on my life once when I realised I didn't have the talent to make it sound that way for other people.'

She looked up and found Sarah watching her intently before she said, 'You put it so well. I studied it for years and years myself. Do you still play?'

'No. Oh well, only socially when someone else wants an accompaniment. Everyone at home plays something, but I think my brother Billy is the most naturally talented of us all. He plays the guitar. We used to harmonise sometimes. I remember once,' she laughed, 'Billy can put on this high soprano voice and my voice is quite deep, and we got conned into doing that— There's a hole in my bucket, dear Liza—in a church concert with him wearing a wig and playing Liza and me as Henry. We brought the house down.' She sobered suddenly and added abruptly, 'I miss them.'

'Nick likes music,' Sarah said gently. 'He has a magnificent collection of classical records.'

Miranda was silent as she recalled the one and only

time she had played a record of Nick's. 'Yes, I know,' she said then. 'I must get them out one day.' She didn't go on to explain that the only reason she hadn't done so before was because of a strange feeling of hurt that Nick hadn't bothered to mention his love of music to her, although after that day he must realise she shared it.

She looked up as Sarah said, 'I wonder if the old piano is tuned?'

If it isn't, Miranda told herself later in the day, I'll get it tuned. Because I might have just struck a spark . . .

But it was ironic, she thought a few days later, that the spark should become a definite crack in Sarah's icy containment not over music but over Miranda's clothes. And that it was instrumental in causing Nick and Miranda's first marital row.

It all started out quite simply with a small dinner party Nick announced he was giving for a colleague who was going to America. Miranda started her preparations several days beforehand and decided that she would get herself a new dress. She felt a thrill of pleasurable anticipation particularly as she didn't have to worry about money this time.

But this small thrill changed to sheer delight, hastily concealed when Sarah wandered into the kitchen and on discovering what Miranda was doing, said thoughtfully, 'What are you going to wear?'

Miranda considered. 'I thought I might go shopping,' she said. 'Do you think I should get a long dress or a short one?'

Sarah made a few more enquiries about the dinner party and who was coming and then said slowly, 'I could come with you if you like. I know a few boutiques . . .' She purposefully rinsed her hands and said, 'How about right now?'

And in a few short hours she had found she had achieved two objectives. She had acquired a dream outfit and she had managed to break right through Sarah's sad preoccupation with herself. But then when they were home again, she could see the effort had tired Sarah and she wasn't surprised when the other girl disappeared to her own part of the house and she knew she wouldn't see her again that day.

'Never mind,' she consoled herself aloud. 'It's a start. A great start!'

'What is?'

Miranda jumped. 'I didn't hear you come home, Nick!'

'I know,' he remarked with a faint grin as he threw his jacket across a chair and loosened his tie. 'I've been home for a good ten minutes. Do you always talk out loud to yourself?' he added as he unbuttoned his sleeves and pushed them carelessly up his forearms, before walking across to pour himself a drink. 'Want one?' he queried over his shoulder.

'Yes, thank you. I guess I must, but I don't really realise it. It's supposed to be a sign of craziness, isn't it?' she said with a smile lurking at the corners of her lips as she accepted the glass from him.

He laughed and cast himself down on to the settee opposite her. 'Supposedly. I don't quite know how you categorise eating the daisies.' He stretched and flexed his shoulders. 'What have you been doing all day.'

'Oh . . . this and that,' she said lightly. I'm not going to tell him about Sarah just yet, she thought. I don't want him to get his hopes up prematurely. 'Aren't you home early?' she asked.

'A little. I bought you a surprise. It's on your bed. Why don't you go and try it on? I'll wait here for you.'

Miranda felt a sudden premonition. 'What is it?' she

asked warily, and added a silent prayer, don't let it be what I think it is!

'See for yourself,' he said lazily with his head resting comfortably on the back of the chair and his long body sprawled out.

She set her drink down carefully.

It was a dress, laid out on their bed. A beautiful black cocktail dress.

She stared at it and closed her eyes briefly. Then, unable to resist it, she picked it up gently and held it up against herself. Now what am I going to do? she pondered as she searched her reflection. I'll just have to tell him ...

'Nick,' she hurried back into the lounge with the dress in her arms. 'Thank you very much, it's beautiful,' she said hastily. 'But I can't wear it tomorrow.'

He sat up abruptly. 'Why the hell not?'

'Because ... I've bought one myself, you see ...' Her voice trailed off uncertainly at the sudden look of anger in his eyes. And her tongue seemed to tie itself in knots as she tried to go with her explanation. 'You see ... it's like this, I mean.' She took a step backwards as he stood up in one swift, fluid movement to tower over her alarmingly.

'Miranda,' he said softly, 'I don't care if you've bought yourself fifty dresses. I can well imagine them too. But this isn't the local Goondiwindi hop tomorrow night, so you'll wear my dress. Do I make myself clear?' He spoke coldly but with unmistakable menace.

And Miranda felt something snap within her. After him saying that to me, she thought burningly, I'm damned if I'll explain anything to him! Why, he's no better than his dear sister Lilian. Oh!

She gritted her teeth and narrowed her eyes in an effort to stay calm. 'Very clear,' she said icily, but felt her teeth chatter in her suppressed rage, and then the lid blew off her anger and hurt. 'So c-clear,' she stammered finding it hard to articulate, 'you give me only one choice.'

The filmy black material gave way surprisingly easily, or perhaps it was the strength of her fury that enabled her to rip the dress apart from neck to hemline. Or perhaps it had been more of an effort than she thought as she found herself panting and sobbing at the same time as she hurled the dress from her. 'I've had all the taunts I can handle!' she breathed. 'Because that was the last straw, you see. Just think how happy your sister will be, Nick—your sister Lilian, when she finds out you're not going bush any longer. And you can tell her from me I heartily wish her up a gumtree! Both of you,' she added distractedly. 'Goodbye!' she hurled defiantly over her shoulder, and stumbled across the room.

'Where do you think you're going, Miranda?' he shot at her as he caught up with her easily just as she reached the front door and swung her round to pinion her against it.

'Back to the bush. Where else? And if you don't let me, I'll scream this house down, Nick, I swear!'

'No, you won't,' he said very quietly, his eyes resting intently on her trembling lips. 'At least not just yet,' he amended.

She turned her head away convulsively and fought him dementedly, but he only laughed at her deep in his throat and finally picked her up in his arms as if she was a child and carried her through to the bedroom to fling her on to the bed.

She lay there fighting for breath and watched him as he deliberately unbuttoned his shirt, with wide wary eyes—watched the slip and flow of the muscles of his shoulder as he threw the shirt across the room and bent to take off his shoes.

Then she closed her eyes and gritted her teeth. There's only one way I can fight him, she thought. Let's see if he enjoys making love to a stone statue. Let's see if he enjoys raping me!

She could never afterwards pinpoint when she knew her plan wasn't going to work. She certainly lay like a limp rag doll while he undressed her carefully, lay with her eyes tight shut as he lifted her into his arms across his body so that her head hung over one arm and her hair streamed over the edge of the bed.

I could have done it too, she often thought afterwards, if he'd been ruthless and brutal with me. But he wasn't. He was too clever for that . . .

But at the time all she could think of were his fingers on her throat just stroking her very delicately, tracing the path from behind one ear to the curve where her neck met her shoulder, tantalising her until the rest of her body seemed to be screaming with frustration and she moved once convulsively in a last desperate bid to escape him.

But his arms tightened momentarily until she was still and his fingers started their quiet caressing again.

Her eyes flew open then to stare up into the dark depths of his and she knew she was beaten. Her body had surrendered for her, her breasts swelling and her nipples hardening.

And my mind? she found herself wondering torturedly as Nick lowered his head to tease her lips gently apart. I don't think I have one . . . She raised her arm slowly and let her own fingers trail across his shoulders and felt a flame, the intensity of which she had never yet felt consume her, so that she became a thing of quicksilver in his arms, wild and provocative, to match his lovemaking step for step like an instrument of abandoned desire she had never thought she would really be. Until she heard him groan her name over

and over again and they were joined in a final unbelievable rapture.

It was some time before they got their breath back
and they lay side by side, their thighs just touching.

'Miranda?' Nick said huskily at last, staring up at
the ceiling.

'. . . Yes?' she managed to whisper.

'I was right—you were made for this.'

She burst into tears.

CHAPTER NINE

'MIRANDA?' Nick said again, wryly, and pushed himself up on to one arm. 'That was a compliment,' he added gravely but with lurking laughter deep in his eyes as he smoothed the tears on her cheek with two fingers.

'Well, it wasn't the one I wanted to hear,' she sobbed, and turned away from him.

'Then you must be different from most women,' he observed.

'Yes, I am. I'm a freak! I thought that's how we got into this argument,' she said tearfully.

'I'm sorry. I shouldn't have said what I did—about your clothes, I mean.' He reached out and traced the curve of her hip. 'Come with me, Miranda.'

She twisted back to look up at him, but he just smiled at her hot, tear-streaked face and held out a hand to her. 'I know just what you need,' he said after a moment as she put her hand into his hesitantly, not sure what he meant.

And she was still unsure when he led her into the en-suite bathroom, into the shower, and stepped in with her. She gasped as the needle-sharp spray gushed over them, soaking them both from head to toe, and her eyes widened despite the water as Nick reached for the soap and using just his hand, lathered her generously and slowly and then did himself, but much more briefly.

'How does that feel? Better?' he asked teasingly, and reached for the hot tap to turn it off.

Miranda squeaked as the water turned cold and he

turned it up full blast. 'Oh!' she gasped, and moved precipitously, only to end up in his arms.

'Better?' he said insistently. 'No more tears?'

'N-no,' she said quaveringly as the water streamed over them. 'I think they've frozen!'

His teeth gleamed whitely against his tan and he lifted her out of the shower and stood her on the bathmat. 'Here,' he kissed her on the lips and handed her a towel. 'Give yourself a brisk rub, you'll feel good.'

He wasn't wrong, she discovered. Her skin felt alive and glowing. She rubbed her hair and turned to find him waiting for her at the door.

'Come on,' he said again, and took her hand. 'I bought you something else too. Try it on.'

She hadn't noticed the sheer, shaded green garment lying across the chair. She stared at him with her lips parted as its soft folds fell about her body and then looked across at herself in the mirror, noting the way the bodice clung to her breasts, emphasising the swell beneath and all but exposing the top half.

'Is it a dress?' she asked.

'A very private one,' he said on a suddenly dry note. 'You'd create a riot if you went out anywhere in it. It's just to wear when we're alone. Like now,' he added, and reached into his closet for a pair of jeans. 'I thought we might have supper in here. No, you relax. I'll get it.'

Miranda sank down on to a chair and waited. She tried to school her mind to blankness, but found it impossible. Sometimes I don't know whether I love him or hate him, she thought with despair. How can I know? It's like loving two different people. Loving the person he is now but how he was earlier—more to the point, *why* he was like that earlier.

She rubbed her brow with her finger tips distractedly. Because he doesn't love *me*, her mind told her. He's never pretended he has. And if that's the case, can this passion last?

She jumped as the door opened and he pushed a trolley in laden with food and a bottle of wine in a silver cooler.

'A midnight feast,' he said seriously, 'for all it's not midnight yet. Hop back to bed. There's a very good chilling movie on tonight.'

He flicked off the overhead light and switched on the television that stood in the corner.

Miranda obeyed and stared at the dishes he placed on the bed. 'That's half my dinner party food,' she said involuntarily.

Nick grinned at her as he poured two glasses of wine. 'I could have cooked,' he said with a quirk to his lips, 'but this was quicker. Besides, you're a much better cook than I am. Comfortable?' he added.

She nodded.

It was a little unreal, she thought later, much later. They had watched the news eating desultorily and sipping their wine. Their supper was a rather unusual combination—cold chicken, ham and asparagus. She had cooked the chicken a day early and had planned to dice it with the ham and asparagus tomorrow and combine it with a cheese sauce as a filling for savoury crepes.

There go my hors d'oeuvres, she thought. I'll have to think of something else.

Nick had added his own touches to the platter between them—sweet golden pineapple rings, marascino cherries and nestling rather artistically in crisp lettuce leaves, juicy wedges of tomato, pink salmon and dark green chopped gherkins. Warm rolls completed that portion of the feast. Her mocha soufflé and homemade ice-cream rounded it all off nicely.

'I'm going to have an awful lot of work tomorrow,' she grumbled as she eyed the soufflé.

'Why?' he asked innocently. 'There's enough here for at least a dozen people.' He slid a silver spoon into the smooth decorated surface and neatly served two helpings.

'Have you ever been to a dinner party where they've presented the dessert with bites out of it?' she asked.

He shrugged and grinned. 'Don't present it. Dish it up in the kitchen. Have you seen this movie before?' he said as the titles slid across the screen.

'Er . . . no.' She licked her lips and decided her mocha soufflé was rather good. 'Have you?'

Nick shook his head and reached for the wine. 'I'm told it's a real thriller, though.'

It was, and as it progressed Miranda found herself holding his hand unconsciously as she stared at the television almost pop-eyed. She didn't notice the way his eyes roamed quizzically over her once as she watched with bated breath. And when it was finished she shivered and turned to him with a grimace.

'I might have nightmares after that!'

'No, you won't,' he drawled as they cleared the remains of their feast together.

'How can you be so sure?'

'Well, you won't be alone in the dark, for one thing. You can hold my hand until you go to sleep if you like.'

But it turned out to be more than that. For the first time in their relationship, Nick gathered her into his arms to sleep and they lay together relaxed and comfortable. And Miranda found she felt like crying.

He moved his chin on the top of her head and said quietly, 'Would you like to tell me now why you didn't want to wear my dress? It occurred to me there might be another reason.'

When did it occur to you? she longed to ask, but couldn't frame those words.

Instead she said, 'Why did you think that?'

'Because you don't make a fuss over nothing,' he said after a small hesitation. 'Not usually, that is,' he added.

Did I? she thought, and moved within the circle of his arms. Maybe I did. And maybe it's all building up inside me like a volcano ... No! I can't let it! This isn't for real. This is ...

'It's Sarah,' she said gruffly. 'She helped me choose a dress for tomorrow night, and all the accessories. For a couple of hours today she forgot all her problems and ... sort of took me under her wing as if I was a lame duck. And that's not all. Do you know, she loves music? I think if I go about it very carefully I can sort of work on that.'

'I see,' said Nick at last. 'So as well as having me patronise you, you had Sarah too.'

'Oh no! It wasn't like that at all,' Miranda protested. 'I invited her help deliberately—I mean, without letting her know it. Do you know what I mean?'

'As part of your plan of rehabilitation? Yes, I see,' he said dryly.

'Wasn't it a good idea?' she asked cautiously after a moment.

'It was a very good idea. Anything that draws her out of herself is. I just,' she was sure he was smiling wryly as he spoke, 'rather enjoyed buying you clothes. But it seems it's a pleasure I shall have to forgo,' he finished lazily.

Miranda could think of nothing to say, and it was he who broke the silence.

'Do you think she'd like to come to the dinner tomorrow night?' he asked abruptly.

Miranda hesitated. 'I'm not sure. Does she know them all?'

'I don't think so. Only David Mackenzie. And we've

both known him for years.'

'He might be an unpleasant reminder to her.'

'Mmm. Although she seemed to get along better with him than any of the other doctors. He's a fair bit older than she is, maybe that's why.' She felt him shrug in the darkness.

'How much older? Is he married?'

'Well, about fifteen years, I guess. And he's a widower. He might be a sort of father figure to her. Why don't you see if you could persuade her, Miranda?'

'I'll try,' she promised. 'But don't count on it. She's really on the alert for ... being pushed around, I think.'

They didn't speak after that. And she lay very quietly in his arms, afraid to break the spell almost, until his deep breathing told her he had fallen asleep. She tried childishly to will herself to stay awake so that she could savour every last moment of this precious peace and serenity she felt. But she drifted off imperceptibly nonetheless.

The dinner party was unexpectedly successful.

And that Sarah attended was through no plotting on Miranda's part but a very genuine bout of nerves which assailed her unexpectedly, late in the afternoon. I've been daydreaming all day, she told herself in exasperation as she looked wildly around the kitchen. Nothing's ready, nor is it likely to be, because all I want to do is run away and hide! The last thing I feel up to is being scrutinised by six strangers! I mean, it's bad enough, keeping up with Nicholas Barrett, without having to do it publicly. Especially when I'm in such a terrible mess...

She reached up to a tall cupboard to lift down an ornate casserole dish and brought down a shower of miscellaneous objects, some glass which shattered noisily on the kitchen floor while the others bumped and rolled around making a cacophony like a brass band.

'Oh no!' she muttered in exasperation as she realised the lid of the casserole had been smashed too. She searched her mind for the choicest words her brother had used and said each lingeringly and feeling, then sank down on to the kitchen stool and burst into tears for the second time in as many days.

'Miranda? What's happened?' Sarah stood anxiously at the kitchen door eyeing the mess.

'I'll never be ready for this dinner party,' Miranda sobbed into her hands. 'That's what's happened! And I don't want to be! I feel like a prize heifer going to be led around a ring. I know what they'll all be thinking,' she groaned dismally.

Sarah hesitated briefly, then she said gently, 'What you need is a hand. Between the two of us we can whizz through this. Then you can have a long soak in the bath and you'll feel much better, you'll see.' She rolled the sleeves of her blouse up as she spoke and stepped carefully into the kitchen. 'I'm not as useless as I look,' she added with a wry grin as Miranda's eyes widened.

'Th-thank you,' she stammered. 'I don't quite know how I got into this mess. I guess it's because I feel so nervous about it all.'

'Honey, with Nick by your side——' Sarah began gently, then her eyes narrowed as Miranda tensed visibly. She paused, then said, 'I think I understand. How would it be,' she said slowly, 'if I came to this dinner party too? To provide moral support as a member of the family who's grown genuinely fond of you, Miranda?'

Miranda caught her breath as she stared into the older girl's dark eyes which were so like her brother's.

'You mean . . . show them that you don't all disapprove of me?' she asked shakily.

'I sure do,' said Sarah with unusual feeling.

'Well, I'd love it,' Miranda said honestly. 'But . . . I mean . . . I don't want you to . . .' She trailed off helplessly.

'My dear, it's the least I can do for you,' Sarah said quietly. 'And don't worry about me. I can cope. Now,' she turned around and surveyed the chaotic kitchen and chuckled with genuine amusement, 'perhaps if you take one end and I take the other . . .'

So what had looked like being a disaster for Miranda became a small success. Nick rang through to say that he had been detained in court and not to expect him much earlier than the guests. This gave both her and Sarah a much needed breathing space.

Miranda said with a definite note of relief in her voice as she put the phone down, 'He won't need to know what an idiot I was now.' She pulled a comical face.

'When he sees you in that dress, he'll be bowled over anyway,' Sarah said practically. She looked at Miranda assessingly. 'Why don't you wear your hair up?'

'Not me,' Miranda answered ruefully. 'My hair has a mind of its own. I'd be shedding bobby pins into the soup and clips into the dessert.'

'If you let me do it for you, you wouldn't,' said Sarah.

'There—do you like it?' she asked some time later as Miranda sat before her dressing table and stared at herself in the mirror.

'I love it,' Miranda said slowly as she raised her fingers to her head. 'It looks natural, sort of. Not strained back.' She fingered the fair stray wisps that framed her face. 'I love it, but will it stay up?'

'Not if you fiddle with it too much,' Sarah said with a laugh. 'But with a bit of hair spray and provided you don't go leaping about the place tonight, I guarantee it. Who cuts it for you? It has a nice line.'

'Er,' Miranda said mischievously, 'do you really want to know?'

'Why not?' Sarah cocked her head to one side and their eyes met in the mirror. 'Don't tell me you cut it yourself?' she asked with a slow smile.

'I thought it was obvious.'

'Not at all,' Sarah said, still laughing. 'The joke's on me. My goodness, I take my hat off to you, Miranda,' she added obscurely. 'I really do. I'd better get myself changed!'

There was a strange look in Nick's eyes as he walked into the house about five minutes before the guests arrived to find the two of them in the lounge. He stopped for a moment and just looked at them both.

'Well, well,' he drawled as he switched his eyes from Sarah to Miranda and took in the upswept hair and the beautifully demure yet clinging smoky grey dress she wore that made her eyes look somehow greener.

Their eyes locked and in that instant she remembered what the designer of the dress had said to her and Sarah when she had tried it on in a superbly elegant boutique. It invests you with a subtle mystery, my dear, he had said. Far more effective than something strapless or backless. It will make some man want to tear it off you, I'm sure . . .

She swallowed suddenly and Nick spoke at last.

He said quietly, 'If I were a painter, I'd want to paint you two side by side. You both look very lovely.' He had crossed to Sarah and dropped a light kiss on her forehead that somehow said more than words could have.

The rest of the evening passed like a whirlwind,

Miranda thought. And, conscious of being dressed right and with Sarah there, she managed to say all the right things and her dinner went without a hitch. Although Sarah did whisper in her ear at one stage that she feared a cat or something had got to the mocha soufflé and should she serve it?

Miranda rose hastily, only being seated at Sarah's insistence that she would share the serving.

'It was Nick,' she said with a giggle. 'I forgot. We'll have to dish it up here in the kitchen. It's going well, isn't it?' she asked, unable to keep a note of joy out of her voice. 'At least they're not all walking around me lifting up my feet and inspecting my teeth!'

She noticed with surprise that Sarah looked rather grim.

'Are you feeling all right?' she asked tentatively.

'I'm fine, Miranda,' Sarah said decisively as she ladled mocha soufflé out. 'I was thinking of Lilian, actually . . . just as well she's not here, otherwise I'd ladle some of this right over her!'

'I'm so tired!'

Miranda coloured as she realised she had uttered her thoughts aloud. They had just seen off their last guest, David Mackenzie. 'I like him,' she added. 'You feel as if you could put your life in his hands. At least I do.' She yawned as Nick and Sarah exchanged a grin.

'Bed for you, my dear,' said Nick. 'I think you've had a big day.'

Miranda caught Sarah's eyes and was surprised to see her sister-in-law close one slightly in just a suspicion of a wink.

'She did you proud, Nick,' Sarah said a moment later. 'And as for being tired—I know how you feel. See you tomorrow, folks!' And she drifted out on to the verandah.

'How did you manage it?' Nick asked with a trace of wonder in his voice.

'I didn't,' Miranda murmured. 'At least . . . well, I'll tell you about it one day,' she added.

He smiled at her and reached for her hand. 'Come along,' he said. 'You'll fall asleep on your feet.'

But as she undressed slowly she found she felt a little . . . unfinished seemed to be the best description. Weary but still keyed-up somehow. She sank down on to the duchess stool in her nightgown and started to unpin her hair. Then she reached for her hairbrush. As she brushed she stared at the room reflected in the triple mirrors. It was spacious and high-ceilinged with beautiful solid furniture and a faded rose pink carpet and hangings. But for all its air of bygone elegance it was the nicest room she had ever lived in.

She put her brush down with a sigh and switched off the lamp beside her. That left only one lamp burning beside the bed. She glanced towards it, quite sure Nick must be asleep already, but was suddenly arrested. He was lying with his arms behind his head, yet there was nothing sleepy about the way his dark eyes rested on her.

Perhaps I'm dreaming, she thought as she stood in the middle of the carpet quivering slightly like a tightly drawn violin string. He hasn't made a move or said a word. Perhaps I'm reading it all wrong . . . because I feel so strange myself.

She stood there supremely unsure and feeling totally confused, because it seemed to her that for the first time he had surrendered the lead to her.

Or is it only my tired, overwrought imagination? she wondered. And can I take a risk of making a fool of myself?

Why not? an inner voice prompted. Why not go for

broke? Your instincts have been right before. Why not make this a time to remember, even if you are only Miranda Smith that was? No, she thought, still Miranda Smith really. A temporary wife . . . but hopelessly in love for all that. She stood there, unaware of how her green eyes reflected her dilemma.

Then her hands seemed to come up involuntarily to untie the lacing of her nightgown at her throat. It crumpled at her feet with a sibilant whisper and she moved forward to kneel at the side of the bed, her eyes wide and searching.

And Nick never said a word, but gathered her into his arms and made love to her gently as if she was rare and precious and breakable.

CHAPTER TEN

MIRANDA felt as if she had turned some corner when she woke the next morning—late, as it turned out, for Nick had already left for work. So she lay in bed examining this new feeling, trying to get it into perspective and wondering if he knew by now how much she loved him. But the thought of last night made her shake off the faint feeling of disquiet this brought to her and she gave herself up to daydreaming.

Later in the morning, she noticed Sarah looking at her curiously now and then, but it was some time before it struck her that the joy she couldn't suppress in her heart must be showing in her eyes.

But she found, as the high summer days ran by like some quiet river, that faint feeling of disquiet had not been a fanciful delusion. Because her relationship with Nick didn't change. It was still that curious blend of aloofness and togetherness. They were just like two friends outwardly, and she began to dread the day when Sarah forgot herself sufficiently to put into words the odd speculation that was sometimes visible in her lovely dark eyes as she watched her brother and his wife together. And although Miranda didn't realise it, the joy died out of her own eyes, like a candle snuffed before it had a chance to burn, to be replaced by a look of defence almost.

Yet if she was inwardly bitter about not having broken through that invisible barrier between herself and Nick, she couldn't deny that Sarah was very close to turning her own corner. She was visibly coming out of her shell of misery and despair and steadily losing that tortured look, and Miranda rejoiced lovingly for her.

They spent a lot of time together, pottering around the garden, tinkering at the piano, listening to music, and they joined forces to persuade Nick to have the swimming pool cleaned and renovated. Not that he had needed much persuading, and they got into the habit of swimming together each evening as the sun went down on the subtropical heat of Brisbane.

Sarah only ever made one mention of the man who had rejected her so painfully. It was while they were watching a play on television about a married man who fell in love with a younger woman and then abandoned her, pregnant, to return to his wife and family. She got up abruptly and switched off the television before the play was finished, and something in the taut way she stood staring out over the darkened garden alerted Miranda.

'Sarah?' she said questioningly.

It was some time before Sarah turned to her to say slowly, 'Yes, Miranda, that's how it was. Only I didn't have comfort even of being a naïve teenager like she was.' She gestured to the television. 'I was . . . thought I was a woman of the world.' She shrugged.

'And the baby?' Miranda whispered.

'I lost that too. I miscarried. I thought . . . at the time I thought, I can't even do that right.'

They never spoke of it again, but it was as if from that moment they were joined by an invisible thread, a sort of a sistership that needed no words. It was also not long after that when Sarah began to worry about her sister-in-law as Miranda had feared.

But when it came, Miranda didn't immediately realise it for what it was.

She was baking and Sarah was flipping idly through a magazine unashamedly licking the bowl.

'Ah,' she said as she glanced at the picture of a red-cheeked bouncing baby, 'now I wonder,' she looked at Miranda through her lashes, 'when we can expect the patter of little feet down these ancestral halls? The last were mine, you know,' she added conversationally.

Miranda wiped her hands on her apron and felt a slight extra heat prickle her skin. But she said practically, 'Give us time, we've only been married three months!' She picked up a cloth and opened the oven door.

'Ah!' Sarah said again. Then, seriously, 'I'm glad to hear you say that.'

'Oh. Why?' Miranda asked, still not seeing the trap.

'Because I had an odd sort of a feeling you and Nick might not be going to have children.'

Miranda turned away suddenly and thought, there! It's out at last and I didn't even see it coming. Just walked straight into the trap. But how can I tell her? How can I tell her he really only married me to help her . . .?

She busied herself at the sink and tried desperately to think.

'What gave you that strange idea?' she managed to say thoughtfully at last.

Sarah didn't answer directly. Instead she said, 'I think you'd make a great mother, Miranda. If the way you've treated me is any guide.' She smiled slightly at Miranda's suddenly wary look.

'What do you mean?'

'Dear Miranda,' Sarah said warmly, 'I may be a lot of things, but I'm not quite blind. You've led me along like a little child since I came to stay here.'

Miranda stared at her. 'Did you . . . did you mind?' she stammered.

Sarah closed her eyes. 'Mind?' she said huskily. 'Oh, Miranda, if only you knew how grateful I was!' She opened her eyes and there were tears on her lashes. 'I don't know how you did it, but in two short months you've taught me how to live again. How could I mind?'

'I didn't do much.'

'Well, I disagree,' said Sarah with a catch in her voice. 'But apart from that you were the only person who didn't pry and probe, didn't try to . . . bring me to my senses by remonstrating with me, didn't try to make me feel as if it was part of my life I should cut out and bury somewhere—as if I ever could!' She paused. 'It's difficult to explain, but I had the feeling you knew—you understood what it's like to fall so helplessly in love so that you feel you can't even breathe on your own. No one else understood that,' she said quietly. 'They wanted me to deny it had happened to me, as if it had been someone else in my skin perpetrating a temporary insanity. But you . . . somehow you gave me the strength to live with it.'

'I think you're right,' Miranda said hesitantly, and stopped conscious of a sudden strange thought. It seemed she had discussed everything under the sun with Sarah, but never Nick. So how did she know?

She caught her thoughts at Sarah's look of enquiry. 'I mean you can't pretend it never happened or be ashamed of it. And it will probably always hurt some. But it's not the *whole* of your life. There's room to grow from it . . . I think.'

They stared at each other.

'I know that now, thanks to you, Miranda,' Sarah said softly at last. 'You seemed to have passed on a secret formula. I don't think I'll ever lack the courage to live again. And if I get depressed and . . . faint-hearted I'll think of you and all the obstacles you've surmounted like a bright beacon, and . . . and if there are more for you, my dear, I'd count it an honour, if you'd let me help you.'

She knows, Miranda thought amidst her undeniable joy for her sister-in-law as she hugged her warmly and they both shed a few tears. She knows.

It stayed with her, that thought, for days, catching her unawares and pouncing on her. Or just sliding across her mind. She knows he doesn't love me. But then it wouldn't be that difficult to work out, living with us as she is. I wonder if she knows why he married me, though? Oh, I hope she never finds that out.

A couple of days later Sarah dropped a bombshell at the dinner table.

'Nick,' she said, 'I've got a job.'

His surprise was clearly evident, but he contained it admirably as Sarah went on to explain. It seemed she had been accepted as the Queensland correspondent for a southern newspaper.

'I'll have a weekly column—you know, local politics and that kind of thing. Which means I'll really have to be on my toes and out and about gathering news like a busy little bee. What do you think?'

'My dear,' he said at last looking down at his plate, 'I don't think I have to tell you.' His voice was curiously uneven and Miranda felt a lump in her throat as he lifted his eyes at last.

'You do realise who's worked this small miracle, don't you?' Sarah went on softly. 'Two people I think I'm fondest of in the world. I can't thank you both enough,' she added gruffly, and raised her wine glass to Nick and Miranda in turn. 'I've also . . . don't think I want to do this, but I have to, and I hope you'll understand . . . I've rented a small flat for myself, not far away, because I have to prove my independence now. Do you see?' she asked Miranda anxiously. 'I'd love to go living here with you two, but I have to . . . put myself to the test.'

Miranda put her hand over Nick's as he moved restlessly. 'We understand,' she said quietly. 'But you'd better come and see us as often as you can, because we're going to miss you.'

Did I ever speak the truth! Miranda mused the day after Sarah left. What am I going to do with myself? And worse, just where do I stand right now?

She stared out over the garden and shivered suddenly. Perhaps it was her imagination, but the sun didn't seem to have as much strength. Not so surprising, though, she thought a moment later. Winter can't be that far away. Will winter see Nick's ardour cooling, I wonder?

She shook herself impatiently. Why think such gruesome thoughts? she scolded herself. It's not going to help when the crunch comes. Be happy for now, Miranda.

Or be like an ostrich . . .

'Damn!' she muttered forcefully. 'It seems I'm very good with other people's problems and quite hopeless with my own.'

But later, some time later, it seemed to her as if that first tinge of autumn she had felt the day after Sarah left had heralded when things began to go wrong.

As the days grew shorter, Nick seemed to be working longer hours, she noticed. And then he became involved in a particularly lengthy and sensational court case and he grew tense and irritable so that the hours they did spend together were strained on his part and filled with a sort of wariness for her. She tried to tell herself that it was the incredible pressure he was under and perfectly natural, but in a corner of her heart she couldn't help feeling she was failing him somehow.

Being first and foremost a practical person, though, she set about looking for new ways to ease his tension.

Some of them succeeded. One weekend she suggested driving to the Lamington National Park south-west of Brisbane. They had had the Mountain Lodge almost to themselves for the weekend and the cold, sparkling air, beautiful scenery and birdlife on the forest trails had wrought a small miracle. Nick had relaxed visibly and for those two days while they walked the bush trails and relaxed in front of a roaring log fire at night it was almost as if they were back on their 'honeymoon'.

Another weekend, she persuaded him to take her fishing. They hired a boat and spent a day on the Bay, and despite his protests, he had enjoyed himself and teased her unmercifully because she was, he said, the most dedicated fisherwoman he had ever met. And the unluckiest.

It was Miranda's next project that came unstuck.

She checked the papers carefully and after some thought, made her plan. But she discovered, curiously, that it didn't seem to appeal to her husband too much; discovered it rather shatteringly too on a chilly evening when she had taken the great liberty of booking seats for a play that was a hit, without consulting him first.

She had prepared a special dinner and was dressed in her grey dress when he arrived home. He eyed her thoughtfully as she handed him a pre-dinner sherry and then said curtly, 'Why are you all dressed up?'

She schooled herself not to panic before she told him.

Nick pulled his tie off and cast himself down into a chair. 'What the hell gave you that idea?' he asked sardonically.

'Well,' she said carefully, 'you seem to be working so hard now, I thought it might help you to relax. Everyone's talking about it. It's very witty and clever . . .'

'Who's everyone?' he interrupted caustically. 'Have

you spoken to anyone who's actually seen it?'

'N—no,' she stammered. 'But I've read about it.'

'You shouldn't always believe what you read, Miranda,' he said cuttingly. 'You of all people.'

She put her glass down on the mantelpiece and found her self control slipping slightly.

'What's that supposed to mean?' she asked reasonably calmly, however, but spoiled it by adding with a flash of anger, 'And who, may I ask, am I supposed to talk to about it? Of course,' she went on bitterly, 'perhaps the bus driver or the garbage collector. They *of all people* might be more my level, mightn't they?' She glared at him.

'I didn't say that,' he answered, looking suddenly amused.

'But you might just as well have,' she flung at him, now thoroughly nettled and beyond much good sense. 'Go on! Why don't you come right out with it?'

'Well, I could,' he drawled, sitting up and staring at the cradled glass in his hands, 'but I seem to remember travelling this road once before. Over the little matter of a dress, wasn't it?' He looked up then and there was so much mockery in his dark eyes she felt she could have killed him had she had any sort of weapon close to hand.

Instead she took a deep breath and made an effort to steady herself. 'I only thought you would enjoy it—we would enjoy it. Is it so wrong to want to see a play?' She shrugged and turned away to wonder how her plan could have gone so wrong.

'There's nothing wrong in wanting to see a play. To my mind the error lies in using it as excuse to get all dressed up so you can be seen abroad in the latest creations and mingle with the so-called sophisticates of this life.'

'I didn't think of it like that!' Miranda whirled on

him and found to her horror that she was crying so
that her delicately applied mascara came away on her
knuckles—which made her angrier. 'If they're all like
you, why should I want to mingle with them anyway?'
she flung at him furiously.

'Good,' he retorted, ignoring her taunt, 'because I
don't either. So I suppose you're going to tell me
you've never seen a proper play, then?'

She tried to speak but found she couldn't. It was as
if they were both rushing downstream on their anger,
and she made a valiant effort to cool hers, but his next
words swept her away.

'Or, of course, don't tell me,' Nick went on with
irony, 'I suppose you're something of an expert, having
been the "local belle". Did you play Juliet to Bill
Hartley's Romeo in the church hall? Or perhaps Eliza
to some wandering, jumped-up jackeroo's Professor
Higgins?'

She caught her breath and flew at him with her
hand raised and her eyes liquid pools of green fire.
'*You* . . .!'

'Don't say it,' he drawled as he caught her wrist.
'Your mother wouldn't have approved, I'm sure.'

She froze at the mention of her mother. And found
a measure of sanity returning to her. Her head drooped
and she felt the fight drain out of her. 'Well, you're
right,' she said slowly at last. 'Which is strange, isn't
it? Because I don't think my mother would have
approved of you. Will you please let go of me,' she
added coolly.

He didn't reply but pulled her down on to the settee
beside him and said meditatively as she collapsed in a
flurry of skirts, 'Do you think not? After all, I did
marry you, didn't I?'

Miranda fought with her emotions and found that
her uppermost desire was to tell him he was an arro-

gant, cold-hearted bastard. But if she'd learnt nothing else since she had come to know Nicholas Barrett, she did know what she would be inviting if she pursued this argument recklessly.

And once he starts making love to me, she thought—well, we know what happens then, don't we?

She looked down at his fingers still on her wrist and said gruffly with an inward sigh, 'Yes, you did. Oh!' she clapped a hand to her mouth with wide eyes, 'I've got something in the oven. It'll be burnt to a cinder!' She tried to stand up, but Nick didn't immediately release her wrist.

'Saved by the bell, Miranda?' he drawled with a wry twist to his lips. He lifted her hand and with his free one formed it into a fist. She glanced down at it and shivered because it looked so small and puny. How symbolic, she thought suddenly.

Then she was free and she stood up uncertainly, conscious of how his eyes were roving up and down her with that now familiar glint in their dark depths, and she turned and fled into the kitchen.

She tore up the theatre tickets the next morning and let them flutter into the waste-paper basket. Another touch of symbolism, she thought tartly. Well, I won't make that mistake again in a hurry. I shall just be a good little wife and drown myself in my home and my garden. And providing my man with all the creature comforts I can.

She dropped her head into hands suddenly and felt the tears trickle through her fingers. There must be some reason why I can't get through this brick wall between us, she thought miserably, and added to herself, Now don't start consoling yourself with platitudes, Miranda! It's not good enough to bury your head in the sand like some ostrich and tell yourself just to be happy with what you've got. It's not enough to be just a body and a good cook and housekeeper for him.

She lifted her head and sniffed and rubbed her tear-streaked face. 'Well, it may be enough for him, but it's not enough for me,' she muttered rebelliously. 'And I'm not going to go out without a fight either! After all, just who is he, anyway? Only a man . . .'

Only a man, she repeated to herself as she leant her hot face against the bedroom window. Only a man, but he made you fall hopelessly, desperately in love with him so that you know no other man will stand a chance of replacing him.

She looked wearily out over her beloved garden. But why does he use *those* particular weapons against me? she wondered as she thought of his taunts last night and his taunt about her clothes the night they had fought over the dress. Is it just a heat of the moment thing? And because he's trained to recognise any weakness, does he sense an insecurity I feel and use it? But if I feel insecure it's not because I'm a little more ordinary than his sophisticated friends but because I lack confidence with *him*.

Or does he do it because he's never really revised his first impression of me? she asked herself. And last night, was it because he really doesn't want to be seen out and about with me where his friends and colleagues might be? *Have* I failed him that way?

She stood where she was for a long time drawing a pattern on the window pane and feeling perhaps lower than she had ever felt in her life. Then out of the blue her father's words slid across her mind. She stiffened and felt some of her old resolution flow back. 'I will be a wife to him,' she murmured aloud. 'If I haven't been up to now, I'll do it yet!' But her new-found resolution was sorely tried later that same day when she glanced out of the lounge windows which she was cleaning to see her sister-in-law Lilian stepping out of a sleek little car.

Miranda's mouth fell open and she had to shut it with an audible click. She looked around wildly and groaned. Her excess of emotion earlier had spurred her to a frenzy of house work in an unconscious bid to exorcise all her demons, and she was hot and tired and grubby and the lounge was a mess.

'Oh dear,' she sighed, which was not what she wanted to say at all. 'Oh dear! Well, there's nothing I can do about it, is there? No.'

She opened the front door and for a moment the two of them just stared at each other. Lilian looked superbly elegant and had not a hair out of place. She blinked slightly as she took in Miranda's dishevelment.

'Oh, hi!' Miranda greeted her. 'It's you. Come in. The place is a mess, I'm afraid—I had this urge to do some spring-cleaning. The morning room is perhaps the best place.'

She led the way past the lounge with all the aplomb she could muster.

Lilian spoke for the first time when she was seated opposite Miranda, who was perched on the edge of her chair.

'I would have thought Nicholas would have hired you a maid, Miranda,' she said thoughtfully as she looked around her. 'It's a big house, after all.'

I *am* the maid, Miranda said, but only to herself being, at that moment just so-minded. The sleep-in maid, she thought with a twist to her lips.

'I can manage,' she said out loud this time. 'After all, I've had a bit of experience at it.'

Lilian raised her thin pencilled brows and looked momentarily nonplussed. 'Yes. Well,' she said finally,

'I came to enlist your support, actually. It's our wedding anniversary in a fortnight's time, and I . . . would very much like Sarah to be there.' She stopped and looked at Miranda just a touch cautiously, Miranda thought.

'Then you should ask her,' Miranda said quietly.

'I have,' Lilian said flatly. 'She told me that in future she wouldn't be part of any family celebrations unless the whole family was present.' She stared at Miranda coldly.

'What . . . I don't . . . do you mean me?' she asked, utterly taken by surprise.

'Who did you think I meant?' Lilian asked with just a touch of insolence that annoyed Miranda immensely and reminded her of Nick. But she schooled herself not to betray it as she eyed the older woman narrowly.

'I see,' she said at last. 'Are you sure she wants to come? I mean, I know she's very busy and I don't quite know how she feels about . . . those kinds of things. Parties—I presume it is a party? Do you know what I mean?'

Lilian looked down at her hands. 'She assured me she was up to it, and it isn't so much a party as a family get-together really. And perhaps I should just say this, Miranda—despite our differences we are quite a close family. Rather we were, until recently. And Sarah is genuinely devoted to her nephews,' she added gently.

Miranda digested this silently. 'Look,' she said, 'if you're accusing me of . . . splitting the family up, I think you're being a bit unfair.'

'Oh?' Lilian said idly, and flicked her fingers at an imaginary speck on her skirt. 'Yet it's over you that Sarah has chosen to isolate herself from us, isn't it? I mean, that's what she did say to me. I'm not hard of hearing, you know.'

Miranda gritted her teeth and surveyed her sister-in-law angrily. But Lilian merely returned her glance with a blank sort of indifference that didn't quite cover the flash of hostility in her eyes.

Miranda stood up and walked a few paces away. I can't get through to her, she thought agitatedly. She's made her mind up about me and that is *that*, it seems. So what will it achieve to wrangle with her? Only my own humiliation . . . and what about Sarah?

She turned back and said abruptly, 'It's up to Nick. I'll speak to him. But it can only be a bit of a sham, can't it?' she added candidly. 'I mean, it won't mean I'll like you any more than you'll like me, will it?'

Lilian looked taken aback. Then she looked haughty. 'If you're as fond of Sarah as you claim to be, I should think you could make the effort.'

'Oh, I could,' Miranda said softly, now thoroughly incensed. 'In fact I can be a very good actress when I set my mind to it. I was just wondering about you. Sarah is very perceptive, you know.'

Lilian flushed unbecomingly and stood up herself. 'I don't doubt that for a minute, my dear,' she said venomously. 'I'm sure you're an excellent actress. In fact I think you've missed your calling. When Nick gets over this little infatuation and gives you your marching orders why don't you take it up as a career? But in the meantime,' she went on icily, 'for the sake of my sister, I'm quite prepared to match you every step of the way!'

'Lilian,' Miranda said through her teeth, 'how do you think your precious brother would react if he heard you talking to me this way?'

Lilian shrugged. 'Who knows—it might even bring him to his senses. It might make him realise how he's tearing us apart. And how unhappy this stand she's taking is really making Sarah. I wonder if you've thought about that? I also notice he's not taking you out and about much by the way. It makes me wonder just how long you've got, Miranda. He's a very sophisticated man, you know. He won't be content with this little love nest arrangement for ever, believe me ... So I think I can count on your presence in a fortnight's time, my dear. See you then,' she said carelessly. 'Oh, and don't bother to see me out. I know my way round this place blindfolded.'

'I don't *believe* this!' Miranda muttered as she watched Lilian's car shoot off down the driveway. 'I just don't believe it. All because I married her brother. What am I? A leper or something?' She picked up a brass ornament and with great deliberation aimed it at a peculiarly ugly china figurine on a side table. The figurine shattered in a very satisfying way all over the carpet and for a moment she felt relieved and almost restored. But it didn't last long. Especially as she had to crawl around the carpet under the furniture with the vacuum cleaner to get at all the splinters of china.

Nor was her disposition much improved by the rush she now found herself in to restore the lounge to some kind of order after her spring-cleaning efforts. 'Mad,' she muttered to herself. 'Quite mad! Whoever spring-cleans in autumn? Or gets involved with people like this mob. I must be mad!'

The sound of a car outside brought her up with a jerk and she looked down at her crumpled jeans in exasperation. Then she gritted her teeth and strolled out on to the verandah. Just let him make any snide comments, she thought, just let him dare!

But the spectacle that greeted her eyes brought her up short. A shiny, bright red mini car stood there and Nick unfolded his long length out of it.

Miranda stilled herself in spite of her barely suppressed ire as she took in this spectacle. His car must have broken down or be in for a service, she thought fleetingly, and then stuck out her chin once more as he mounted the front steps.

'Catch,' he said lightly, and tossed her the car keys.

She caught them in a reflex gesture, but only just inches from the verandah floor. 'What's this?' she asked as her body recoiled from its graceful arc.

'It's yours.'

'What is?'

'The car—what else?' he answered leaning his shoulders against the doorframe. 'I'm told bus drivers don't make the most scintillating conversation.'

'Bus . . . drivers,' Miranda said slowly, looking from the keys lying in her palm to the little car.

'Or garbage collectors,' Nick said reflectively.

'Do you mean . . .?' She stopped and looked at him incredulously.

He shrugged and nodded.

'But I didn't mean it that way!' She rushed into speech and then found herself strangely tongue-tied.

'I know you didn't,' he said with a lurking grin. 'Or else I'd have bought you a bus or one of those mechanical monsters that compact the stuff as they go along. You'll have to drive me to work tomorrow,' he added, 'and bearing the magistrate's words in mind, I caution you to give your driving your fullest attention.'

'Nick——' she began pleadingly as she followed him inside, and jumped as he turned round suddenly so that they were only inches apart. 'You didn't have to buy me a car,' she stammered with her head tilted back to look up at him.

'I know. Maybe that's why I did it,' he said obscurely, and then smiled faintly at her look of bewilderment. 'I hope it gives you lots of pleasure,' he added gravely.

She stood on tiptoe suddenly and kissed him. 'Thank

you,' she said shyly. 'I don't really know how to thank
you . . .'

He raised his eyebrows ironically. 'I could think of
one way,' he murmured.

'N—now?' she queried, going red beneath his eyes.
'But I'm filthy!'

'Then let's say a little later, shall we?' He touched
her cheek with his fingers. 'May I make a date with
you, Mrs Barrett? An after-dinner date?'

She nodded wordlessly and thought she might just
die then because she loved him so much.

And it was while she was in the bath that she came
to a decision. She would go along with Lilian for his
and Sarah's sake.

She lay back in the warm scented water feeling
somehow relieved but curious at the same time. What
had he meant earlier about the car? Was he . . . surely
he wasn't going to start heaping her with gifts to take
away with her?

She shivered suddenly and then cautioned herself
not to start leaping to conclusions. After all, didn't she
have a date with him shortly?

She climbed out of the bath in a sudden confusion
of clamouring pulses.

'Nick,' she said abruptly as they ate.

'Mmm?'

'Lilian came to see me today.'

'Well, well,' he said after a moment. 'What for?'

'To invite us to her wedding anniversary celebration.'

'Fair dinkum!' he said, and grinned suddenly. 'Did
you fall down in surprise?'

'Not quite,' she said with an answering grin. 'But,'
she sobered and shrugged, 'I thought maybe for
Sarah's sake we should go. You see Sarah's, from what

I gather, thrown down the gauntlet, sort of threatened to cut herself from Lilian until she accepts me.' She looked up from her plate to find Nick looking at her penetratingly with narrowed eyes and a faint frown.

'I see,' he said quietly at last. 'Is that what Lilian came to tell you? That she was going to accept you?'

Miranda hesitated. 'Yes, that was it,' she said gruffly.

'Do you feel you can accept her, Miranda?' he shot at her unexpectedly.

'Well . . . yes,' she said. 'I mean, there's no reason not to, is there? And besides, I hate the thought of Sarah, and for all I know, you, being cut off from Lilian's children. But I said I'd ask you first,' she added hastily, not quite liking his expression. Oh God! she thought, maybe he really doesn't want me in the bosom of his family or to be seen with me by his friends. And she found her hands were suddenly clammy.

'All right,' he said unevenly. 'Perhaps you're right. Sarah is very fond of the kids. We'll go for her sake.'

Miranda stood up and started to clear the dishes, feeling unreasonably deflated. If only he'd added something! I mean, I know we should do it for Sarah's sake, but . . .

'Miranda.' She looked up as he said her name softly. 'Leave that. Besides you're not dressed for doing the dishes.'

She dropped her hands. 'I . . . I put it on,' she muttered, referring to the shaded green dress she had donned after her bath, his gift to her, 'because you . . . we . . . that is . . .'

'I know why you put it on,' he told her with a fleeting grin and a glance that raked her from head to foot. 'And I can assure you it's achieved the desired effect. If you come over here I'll demonstrate.' He stood up.

Miranda lowered her eyes and felt her heart somersault. How could he do this to her with just a few words? She peeped through her lashes. But he was just standing there tall and straight and strong.

She moved forward slowly until she stood right in front of him. Then she looked down at her hands with her colour fluctuating and feeling almost as shy and frightened as she had the first time.

The first move Nick made was to twine his fingers in her hair and tilt her head back so she had to look into his eyes, which were brooding and sombre, the lids half lowered over their dark depths.

'Tell me you want me, Miranda,' he said so quietly she could barely hear.

I love you! she wanted to cry with every fibre of her being, but she knew she couldn't say it. 'I . . . yes,' she whispered at last.

'Say it, Miranda.'

'. . . I want you, Nick. You must know that,' she whispered.

'All the same, I like to hear you say it,' he said a little dryly, his eyes resting on her trembling lips. Then his hands were moving down the slender column of her neck to her shoulders, but hesitantly, and they hovered before slipping beneath the bodice of her dress as if he was testing his control. And for one fleeting horryifying instant she thought he was going to turn and walk away from her.

But instead with a groan he swept her into his arms and kissed her until she thought she would faint. Then he picked her up in his arms and carried her through to the bedroom.

CHAPTER ELEVEN

THE next two weeks flew by, or so it seemed to Miranda. And for all her own ever-increasing tension at the thought of Lilian's anniversary, between herself and Nick things seemed easier, she thought. As if they had slipped back into the easy camaraderie they had shared when Sarah had been with them and it had been important not to rock . . .

'Not to rock the boat,' she murmured to herself one day as she cleaned and polished her little car. 'Maybe that's what frightens me now. There's no reason for Nick to be afraid of rocking the boat now if he chooses. And yet I'm strangely content for once. Perhaps I was trying *too* hard.'

This idea was reinforced somewhat that same day when, without thinking too much about it, she came across a pack of cards in the bureau drawer and decided to play patience after dinner.

Nick had brought home a bulky briefcase and was sitting in the lounge surrounded by what Miranda assumed were transcripts of evidence. She would have dearly loved to pore over them with him but didn't have the courage to break into his absorbed study of them.

So she set out the cards on the dining room table, tuned her little transistor in softly and promptly lost herself in the game. But after a while the advertisements on the commercial station playing began to get on her nerves, so she fiddled with the knob and stopped it spellbound on a non-commercial station as the golden notes of Litolf's Scherzo poured forth.

She leant back and closed her eyes in pleasure, for

even the slightly tinny sound of her transistor couldn't drown the beauty of it.

'Miranda?'

She came back with a start as the last chord struck and realised it had given goosebumps.

Her eyes focused slowly on Nick and something unusually warm in his eyes prompted her to say, 'I like that so much. I feel as if there's an answering chord in me. I don't mean I could ever write music like that, but I feel as if it's telling me something, do you know what I mean?'

'Tell me,' he said slowly.

She considered. 'As if—it's as if nothing much else is so important. That there's an inner core of oneself that can transcend all your miseries if you'll let it.' She hesitated. 'I feel, if I can listen to that, or I suppose other people see it in paintings or literature, but if it's there it can help you out of the deepest hole you've got yourself into.' She shivered suddenly. 'Fancy having that *power* to stir people so! I suppose that's what you call genius. I never really realised it before.'

'Not many people do,' Nick said soberly. 'You have an uncanny knack of hitting the nail on the head. I don't understand it, but you have it.'

'Do you mean you don't understand the genius bit?'

'No, I don't mean that. I . . .'

'Oh, *I* understand,' Miranda said, wincing inwardly at the sudden hurt. 'It seems strange to you, coming from me. Well, it seems strange to me too . . .'

'Miranda——' he interrupted with a sudden look of compassion, but she gave him no chance to hurt her further.

She asked brightly, 'Have you ever played patience?'

'Yes,' he said after a moment. 'It's a very aptly named game.'

'It is, isn't it? Now a good game of poker!'

She thought for a moment, then she cast him a wicked glance and said gently, 'I reckon I fell out of my cradle knowing how to play poker.'

'Ah,' he said with a flash of amusement in his eyes, and drew out a chair. 'Point taken—did I really say that? I suppose I must have. Well, perhaps you can get your revenge now. What stakes shall we play for?' He grinned at her with that spark of devilry she mistrusted devoutly.

She sat back and eyed him thoughtfully. 'Well, I never play strip poker, if that's what you had in mind.'

Nick laughed at her and said, 'That sounds ominous, my dear. You have a militant look about you that makes me wonder what consequences some poor unsuspecting chap suffered when he offered you those stakes.'

Miranda had to smile herself then at the recollection. 'You've hit the nail on the head yourself,' she said grudgingly. 'He didn't realise I was playing with one of my brothers at the time.'

When Nick stopped laughing he said, 'They've taken it well, haven't they? Your family, I mean. Before I met your father, I quite thought they might organise a posse,' and grinned again at her startled look.

'Let's see,' she said ingenuously some time later. 'You owe me a dollar, I think.'

He eyed her and then grinned. 'Whoever taught you this game knew what they were doing.' He solemnly handed her a dollar. 'We'll have to have a rematch.' He stood up and stretched lazily, looking relaxed, she thought.

Sarah was quite bemused, the first time she and Miranda met after Lilian's visit.

'Do you mean Lilian actually ate some humble pie?' she demanded incredulously.

'Well ... sort of,' Miranda said, and wished she could lie more easily. 'And all thanks to you,' she went on hastily. 'But there was no need to go out on a limb over me, you know,' she added seriously.

'Miranda, there was every need, my dear,' Sarah said intently, and stopped abruptly. 'Are you going?' she asked after a minute.

'Nick seems to think it's a good idea. I thought you might like to help me choose what to wear. Although I could wear my grey dress again. I've only worn it once—well, twice, actually.' Miranda grimaced slightly.

'What's wrong?' Sarah asked.

'Oh, nothing,' Miranda said airily, going faintly pink about the ears. 'But you haven't seen my new toy yet, have you? My new car? Care to come for a spin? Although I must warn you I have one dangerous driving conviction to my credit.'

'I don't believe you,' smiled Sarah.

'Well, I do,' Miranda assured her laughingly. 'That's how I came to meet your brother, didn't you know? He was in court to ... protect the other party's interests or something.'

'Oh dear!' Sarah said with some concern, and added with considerable acuteness Miranda thought, 'Was he very nasty?'

'Well, as it turned out, I myself was the best protection their interests could have had,' she said ruefully. 'So he didn't have anything to say in court. And it was only by accident that I heard him comment afterwards. He wasn't ... kind,' she said dryly.

'I can imagine,' Sarah murmured, then looked uncomfortable. 'I didn't mean ...'

'I know that,' said Miranda.

'Anyway you seem to have made him eat humble pie too, Miranda.'

'I wouldn't put it quite like that,' Miranda said
wryly. 'But listen, shall we go shopping or not? What
do you think?'

Sarah had thought yes and the dress they had chosen
was superb—a smoky topaz colour which made
Miranda's eyes look startlingly green; it was simple in
style, high-necked and with long filmy sleeves and a
gracefully cut skirt that didn't look full until she
twirled around.

But even confronted with her reflection in the mirror
on the night of nights and positive there was nothing
she could do to improve her appearance, she found she
was a bundle of nerves and wishing heartily that she
hadn't talked herself into this celebration.

Nick was late home from work too, which on this
night didn't help at all because it was a rush from the
minute he stepped into the house, and beyond a cur-
sory glance at her and a murmured, 'You'll do,' he
didn't have time to say much more. And when they
were seated side by side in the car, he didn't seem to
want to say much more, just concentrated on his
driving.

So that Miranda sat there forcibly restraining herself
from chewing her fingernails until they finally drew
up in front of a palatial residence set well back in its
grounds and lit up like a birthday cake.

She swallowed as the car came to a halt and cast him
an almost beseeching look, but all he said was, 'Ready?'
and she nodded dumbly.

There were seven people assembled in the superbly
elegant lounge of her sister and brother-in-law's house
as she and Nick entered it. Lilian, in pale lilac that
suited her admirably, standing beside a tall, dis-
tinguished-looking man obviously her husband, and
two fearsomely groomed boys of about twelve and
fourteen, Miranda surmised.

Then there was Sarah in pale green and looking quite ravishing with a drink in her hand and laughing up at David Mackenzie, and Miranda caught her breath because there was something fleeting and unguarded in the doctor's eyes as they rested on Sarah's upturned face.

Oh, I hope so, Miranda found herself thinking fervently. He'd be perfect for her.

But her thoughts faded almost before they could take root as she realised who the seventh person was. Samantha Seymour, seated like a flower on a straw-coloured settee in a dress of almost the same shade that made her hair flame with an exotic warmth and richness.

Miranda knew that the little tableau before her eyes would be frozen in her mind for ever. As indeed for an instant, as she and Nick stood just inside the doorway, everyone seemed to freeze like a photographic still. And then the camera started to whir as Lilian moved forward graciously and Miranda was conscious of but one thought. She said a family gathering. But *Seymour* . . .

'Miranda! Nick, my dear. It's good to see you.'

Lilian took her brother's arm and kissed him affectionately.

'Now who doesn't Miranda know?' she said smoothly. 'This is my husband Lawrence and our sons Peter and Nicholas junior and . . . but I think you already know Lawrence's sister, Samantha, don't you?'

Miranda could never afterwards imagine how she got through the first few minutes of Lilian's anniversary celebration. Because she was only conscious of the shock she felt.

Why didn't anyone tell me? she wondered when she was able to think clearly. Why didn't I work it out for myself? The name—I thought it was just coincidence. No wonder Lilian hates me . . .

She accepted a drink absently and forced herself to appear normal and relaxed, although she had no idea what she said or did because it seemed to her as if there were only three people in the room. Herself and Nick and the woman she knew had hoped to marry him, had loved him . . . maybe as much as Miranda did. Is that why even Sarah never mentioned her and Lilian . . . hates me? she thought miserably. Because I ousted one of the family? How awkward . . . how impossible really, she thought as the celebration swirled and eddied about her like some rich tapestry of colour and light.

And she couldn't help noticing with an added feeling of pain around her heart how delighted Peter and Nicholas junior were in the company of their uncle and aunts assembled together and how happy Sarah looked.

Nor could she interpret the one direct glance she exchanged with Samantha Seymour before dinner as anything but frightening. Because in that one clashing of eyes, Miranda knew that nothing was forgiven or forgotten, and she wondered if Lilian and Samantha deliberately planned this evening.

But even if they hadn't, she realised later, they couldn't but have applauded the way fate played into their hands that night. For just after the party was seated at the long, beautifully polished dinner table an urgent phone-call came through for Nick.

'Oh, my dear!' Lilian exclaimed, sounding genuinely regretful, 'can't it wait until morning, or at least until after you've finished your meal?'

'I'm afraid not, Lilian,' he said with just a trace of impatience. 'What may be a vital new piece of evidence has come up in this case I'm working on. I have to make sure it's thoroughly checked and then we have to work it into our defence for tomorrow. I can't do it on the telephone.'

'But you don't have to do all that yourself?' she objected.

'Fortunately not,' he drawled. 'Not the leg work. So I hope to be able to get back to you pretty quickly, dear sister.' He moved round the table and laid his hand briefly on Miranda's shoulder. 'I'll be as quick as I can,' he said quietly, and was gone before she could express herself.

Which was just as well, she thought as she forced herself to relax. It might have sounded very odd if I'd said, 'Please, don't leave me here . . .'

But as it turned out, for a time anyway, it wasn't such an ordeal. Sarah and David made sure she wasn't left out of the conversation that flowed around the table, and she even found that she couldn't quite carry the aversion she felt for Lilian to her husband Lawrence. Because he too seemed to be making a genuine effort to include her. Although she had another shock not long after Nick left when she discovered through the course of the general conversation that Samantha was in fact a qualified lawyer herself and a junior partner in her brother Lawrence's firm.

So they've probably been seeing a lot of each other, she thought dazedly. And all the time here I was thinking she'd dropped off the edge of the world or something equally silly.

Then there was a small disturbance as Master Nicholas and Peter were shooed off to bed, their time limit having expired apparently, and this caused a lull in the conversation into which Samantha said quite clearly,

'How do you like your new car, Miranda?'

Miranda stared at Samantha, who sat diagonally

across the table from her, in surprise. 'How did you know about it?' she asked before she stopped to think.

'Oh, Nick told me about it,' Samantha said casually, 'one evening I think it was when we'd both worked late and . . . found ourselves in the same coffee bar for a reviver.'

Miranda tensed, for the hesitation seemed to give direct lie to the words 'found ourselves', but it seemed there was worse to come.

Samantha chuckled and contrived to peep engagingly at Miranda through her lashes. 'Can I tell you what else he said?' she asked archly.

'Be my guest,' Miranda said after a moment during which she saw Sarah move restlessly, and she tried to make her own voice easy and unstrained.

'Well, he said,' Samantha looked playfully around the table, 'it's bright red so that everyone can see her coming. Well, of course I said to him that he was nothing but a male chauvinist, but it seems he's not wrong about you, Miranda, is he? He told me all about your little brush with a cabinet . . .'

'*Stop it*, Samantha!' Sarah interrupted hoarsely. 'Oh, I knew this was all too good to be true,' she went on contemptuously as a frozen hush fell over the rest of the table. 'Do you think we all haven't realised you were waiting quietly and oh, so insidiously in the wings, so that it was impossible for Nick not to trip over you every way he turned?'

'Oh, Sarah,' Samantha said pityingly, 'do you honestly think Nick would be tripping over me if he didn't want . . .'

'Samantha!' This was Lawrence, Miranda realised dimly, his voice curt and sharp. 'How dare you! Miranda is a guest in this house, and if you don't like it you may leave. Lilian!' he added peremptorily.

But what he was about to say to his wife was never

uttered, because Miranda intervened herself then.

She stood up carefully and pushed her chair in, then stood with her hands resting on the top of it. I can end this now, she thought with painful detachment and clarity, unaware of how five pairs of eyes rested on her with varying expressions but a look of arrested expectancy common to them all. Because I can't go on tearing this family apart. Can't go on tearing myself apart like this. If he even respected me a little would he discuss me like that with *her* of all people? I thought I could live without his love, but I can't live with this. Yet how to do it, so that I don't leave behind scars among them that will never heal?

She raised her head suddenly and saw the anguish in Sarah's lovely dark eyes and knew suddenly how she had to do it.

'Look,' she said abruptly, 'I can't say I admire or applaud the way some of you have treated me. But I have to admit you're right. Maybe,' she shrugged, 'you're gifted with foresight, I don't know, but Nick and I *are* mismatched, and it didn't take very long for us to discover it.'

'Miranda!' Sarah whispered incredulously. 'What are you saying?'

'It's true, Sarah,' she said gently. 'Of all people you must know it. I think you even tried to warn me once. But you see, for Nick it was something . . . purely physical, and for me,' she shrugged, 'well, I can't deny I was dazzled and it was like an impossible dream come true, but for all that it wasn't very long before I discovered I'd married the wrong man.'

She waited for the shock waves to subside around the table. 'And,' she went on in the same even, almost detached voice, 'if that man could ever forgive me for allowing myself to be swept off my feet, seduced by wealth, sophistication . . . I don't really know what it was, but I guess I was more naïve than most—if he can forgive me, I'm going back to him just as soon as I can.'

'Bill Hartley,' Samantha murmured so that everyone looked at her and Miranda's green eyes flashed sudden fire, but with an effort, she contained herself.

'The same,' she said quietly. 'So you see, there's nothing for you to . . . be divided about. And for you, Sarah,' she said, and winced as she saw that Sarah was crying openly, 'the best way you could repay me for anything I ever did for you, would be to heal the breaches in this family that I . . . rather thoughtlessly brought about.'

It seemed no one was capable of speech, not even Samantha, for once, and Miranda said into the silence at last, 'I . . . I think I'll go now,' with the first unsteadiness her voice had betrayed so far.

'I think that would be a very good idea,' a voice said from the doorway, causing them all to spin round and Miranda at least to feel suddenly faint.

Nick strolled into the room, his face a white mask of fury.

'After you, Miranda,' he said expressionlessly.

CHAPTER TWELVE

MIRANDA stared at him aghast. His eyes glittered strangely and she knew intuitively that most of his rage was directed at her.

She licked her lips and swallowed convulsively. But she knew there was nothing else she could do. And she went with her head held high but her heart beating like a tom-tom.

It seemed as if no one else in the room dared to even breathe as he followed her out and closed the door decisively.

He took her arm in a bruising grasp and led her out to the car.

'Get in,' he said violently.

She got in, although she really felt like running into the night and putting as much distance between them as she could.

He slammed the car into gear and the engine roared in the still night.

'Nick?' she said tentatively.

But he didn't answer, only set the car hurtling along at such a wicked speed that Miranda couldn't help but clutch the armrest and wonder if he meant to overturn them.

Then they were home in no time at all and she could only sit like a frozen dummy until he gritted through his teeth, 'Get out.'

She obeyed and stumbled into the house, her mind refusing to function until they reached the bedroom and Nick pulled open a cupboard and handed her a suitcase from it. 'Now pack,' he said contemptuously,

'I'll pack in my own good time,' she answered slowly, standing at bay. 'I don't need you to tell me when to pack!' She tossed her head defiantly.

'That's strange,' he blazed at her. 'You didn't hesitate to tell *them* you were packing up and leaving—just as soon as you could, I think you said?'

'I . . . you don't understand!' she cried.

'I understand one thing,' he said coldly. 'If you're in such a fever to get back to Bill Hartley I'll deliver you myself, Miranda. Maybe not . . . intacto, as they say, but nevertheless second-hand, well run in at least. Your choice of words, I think,' he added cruelly.

'Oh!' she gasped. 'I . . . you . . .!' But she couldn't speak, she found as the short fuse on her own anger exploded.

She reached for the first thing that came to hand, which turned out to be a heavy silver candlestick, and whirled on him like a wild cat.

But he didn't move, didn't even raise a hand to stop her, just watched her with narrowed, mocking eyes that dared her to do her worst.

She lowered her upraised arm slowly and looked at the object in her hand unbelievingly. Then she put it down very carefully and burst into tears.

Nick let her cry into her hands for about a minute. Then he said roughly, 'Listen to me carefully now, Miranda.' He waited.

She raised her head at last.

'I'll decide when this marriage is over, not you. And if I were you,' he said very quietly but with a wealth of menace, 'I'd accept it. Because if you do anything else to end it before I'm good and ready you'll find yourself living to regret it.'

'B—but . . .' she stammered.

'No buts,' he interrupted implacably. 'And no running away. Because I'll find you like I found you the last time. No,' he agreed sardonically as her eyes widened suddenly, 'I didn't just happen to run into you by coincidence that day.'

'How?' she whispered.

'It doesn't matter,' he said tautly. 'Just bear it in mind for future reference, though,' he added very softly as his eyes roamed her hot, tear-streaked face.

Miranda swallowed nervously and jumped as the telephone on the bedside table shrilled.

'I'll get it,' Nick said cuttingly.

She tensed. But it was obviously a call from his office and after a few curt sentences he dropped the receiver and turned to her.

'Something else has come up,' he said abruptly. 'One way or another this is going to be a long night.' He looked her over thoughtfully. Then he seemed to come to a decision. 'Here's what we'll do. Try and get some sleep now and then as early as you can in the morning, drive down to Burleigh to the unit. That should throw my . . . relatives off the scent for a while,' he added flatly. 'I'm going to seek an adjournment on this case in the light of this new evidence and, I hope I shall be down sometime tomorrow myself. So you better be there, Miranda,' he said with unmistakable emphasis.

'I . . . I . . . look,' she began helplessly.

'Save it for tomorrow,' he said briefly, and reached out to grasp her by the shoulders. 'Just be there.' He stared down into her eyes, his own harder and colder than she had ever seen them.

She shivered and flinched as his grasp tightened. 'You're hurting me,' she whispered.

'I should put you over my knee and really hurt you,' he snapped, then released her suddenly and strode out of the room.

But Miranda stood rooted to the spot seemingly until the last faint sounds of his car faded into the night.

Then she sank down on to the bed and stared at her hands and tried to think.

But as the hours passed if anything she grew more confused. How had Nick tracked her down to Burleigh Heads? And why? Surely it seemed an extreme measure for a girl who *might* be able to help his sister and whom he was passingly attracted to?

The same girl, she reminded herself dully, he saw fit to turn into some kind of a comic strip character and keep doing it right up until the last fortnight.

'It's bright red so they can see her coming . . .'

She winced as she recalled Samantha's words and closed her eyes in pain. I wonder how many coffee bars they found themselves in? she thought, and tilted her head back so that her tears splashed on to the neck of her beautiful topaz dress. But why was he so angry with me? I gave them all the perfect opening. The perfect outlet to dispose of me quickly and quietly. Maybe it's only his ego that's hurt. Maybe he's the kind of man who has to do it himself. Does he feel less a man because I tried to walk out on him, instead of the other way around? And why has he kept me like a prisoner in an ivory tower since we married?

'Oh!' she said out loud, and buried her head in her hands. 'I feel like a . . . mouse you see in a pet shop. Going round and round on one of those silly plastic . . . whatever you call them!'

She got up and paced the room. 'It just doesn't seem to fit,' she murmured despairingly. 'I'd rather be with him than anyone else in the world. But how can I? And more to the point, just how did he find me?'

It was a bleak overcast dawn that greeted her weary eyes. She glanced down at the packed suitcase beside her and then at the keys in her hand. House key, car key, unit key.

But which way shall I go? she asked herself. If I go west there's no way he could wrest me from my father and my brothers or . . . Bill. I mean he wouldn't try to do it by force, surely . . .?

The unit was quite unchanged from her memories of it. The same sense of being suspended above the ocean when you stepped out on to the balcony, the darkly wooded expanse of Burleigh Hill to the right and the same emerald green sheets on the bed. Only the day itself was different. Not the bright sparkling day of her memories but dull with heavy, swollen, lowering clouds.

She dropped her case to the bedroom floor and stared at the bed as if mesmerised. Then she took her shoes off and lay down on it.

Just for a minute, she thought. Just . . . for a little while . . .

She slowly drifted awake.

'Nick?' she murmured, not quite awake as she reached unthinkingly across the bed.

'I'm here.'

The words jerked her upright with a heart-stopping wrench, wide awake now. 'I . . . I didn't hear you,' she stammered as she took in his tall figure framed in the doorway.

'You wouldn't have, you were fast asleep,' he said unemotionally.

'Have you . . . been here long?' Miranda asked self-consciously as she took in the weary set of his shoulders beneath the blue silk shirt and the look of strain in his dark eyes.

He shrugged. 'Not long.'

Nick said nothing more for a moment, then he glanced at his watch and shrugged. 'Not that long. I could do with a drink, how about you?' He turned and walked out without waiting for an answer.

Miranda looked at her own watch and her eyes widened. She had slept for hours and it was now late afternoon. She looked out of the window, to see a magnificent storm raging on the horizon out to sea and a dark diagonal shaft of rain seemingly etched in pencil on a lighter backdrop beneath the thunder clouds. The sea itself was the colour of slate.

She sighed suddenly, unable to name exactly how she felt but knowing that somehow she had to get through to Nick. She had to break down the wall, had to find the strength to leave him without running away like a thief in the night. Had to make him understand— but how?

She slipped off the bed and decided to have a shower and tidy herself up first. Maybe it would help her to think straight.

She took her time about it and then, perhaps deliberately, donned a pair of jeans and a blouse that came from the pre-marriage era of her life before her wardrobe had extended and blossomed. She brushed her hair and tied it back simply with a ribbon. Then she took a deep breath and forced herself to walk into the lounge.

Nick was standing in front of the big picture windows looking out at the storm with a glass in his hand. He didn't turn.

Miranda picked up the glass set waiting for her on the bar and sipped at it. Then she put it down resolutely.

'Nick, you said I could talk to you.'

He didn't move.

'Nick?' she said after a moment.

He looked down at the glass in his hand and then turned. They stared at each other, Miranda searchingly, but all she could see was that he looked tired and drained.

'Did you get your adjournment?' she asked involuntarily. 'I suppose you must have,' she answered her question, a little embarrassed, 'or you wouldn't be here.'

Something flickered in his eyes, but he only said, 'Yes, until after the weekend. Sit down,' he added abruptly.

She hesitated, feeling as if the initiative was slipping from her as it always seemed to do when she was with him. But she followed suit as he cast himself down on to the settee.

'If you're too tired?' she said uncertainly.

'No.'

She started to speak several times and then reached sideways for her drink and took a fortifying sip.

'I don't quite know how to say this,' she muttered with her glass cradled between her hands, 'But,' she took a breath and then said clearly, 'I just can't stay married to you.'

Raindrops splattered against the windows as the storm moved inland, the only sound to break the silence.

Nick spoke at last, sounding quite unmoved and as if he was trying to deal patiently with a fumbling, inarticulate child. 'On account of Bill Hartley?'

'No,' she said, and found herself smiling slightly as she went on, 'Anyway, for all I know he could have decided to marry Shirley Tate by now.'

'I doubt that very much,' he said dryly.

She shrugged. 'Well, you don't know him, so I don't see how ...' She broke off as he lifted his eyebrows ironically.

'You do?' she said bewilderedly. 'But I don't understand.'

'It's quite simple really,' he said readily. 'When you bolted after Sarah slashed her wrist, I drove up to Goondiwindi to see him. That's how I knew you were down here at Burleigh. As a matter of fact I even knew which caravan park you were in.'

'Bill . . . told you?' she said weakly.

'He showed me your postcard.'

Miranda licked her lips as she tried to sort it all out.

'Go on,' said Nick after a moment. 'If it's not on account of Bill Hartley, what are your reasons?'

'Well,' she said trying to steady her voice and still trying to make some sense of what she'd just learned, 'I mean . . . well, there's your family,' she said hurriedly as she looked up to see him studying her thoughtfully. 'Our marriage has just broken them up. I saw it last night. Sarah and Lilian, Lilian and Lawrence, Lawrence and Samantha . . .' She paused for breath and then said steadily, 'I can't do that to them. It's just not worth it for the . . . temporary set-up we've got. Is it? I mean . . .' She lifted her shoulders helplessly.

'Miranda,' he said in a suddenly hard voice, 'we'll deal with the temporary aspect of it, as you call it, in a minute. Just let me say this first—it's none of their business who I marry or how long I stay married, for that matter. But in point of fact *nobody* other than Samantha would have suited Lilian. If I'd married the Queen of Sheba she would have been just as unacceptable to Lilian, because she had her heart set on me marrying Samantha and whoever else it had been, we would have just had to ride out Lilian's disapproval, because I never had the slightest intention of marrying to please *her*. And believe me, Miranda, Lilian wouldn't have cut herself off from me or Sarah for very long if you hadn't played right into her hands. She must have thought all her Christmases had come at once last night,' he said with bitter contempt which Miranda wasn't at all sure wasn't directed at her more than at his sister Lilian.

'So,' he went on, after giving her a chance to speak which she found she couldn't take, 'we've disposed of Bill Hartley, I think, and the family. What's left? Haven't you enjoyed these past few months since we married?' He looked at her searchingly but coldly, she thought.

'It's not that,' she said miserably at last, and couldn't help wondering why, of all people, she had had to choose a barrister to fall in love with, to be having this impossible conversation with.

'Then you're bored or getting that way. Sorry you tied yourself down to one man before you had a chance to play the field, maybe?' he asked with a mocking little smile playing about his lips.

She caught her breath at the flame of anger that licked through her and forgot all her caution as she stood up and said coldly and clearly, 'I was not bored. I was not restless. Nor was I aching to . . . to play the field, and I hate you for saying th—that,' she flung at him, stuttering in her anger. 'But I couldn't help wondering if I was some kind of a freak that had to be kept in the background like some mongrel you wouldn't dream of taking to the dog show! And talking of playing the field . . . well, it seems you're a fine one to talk! You might not have married her, but it didn't seem to stop those amusing little chats you kept having with Samantha about dear Miranda . . . dear me, she's always worth a laugh, isn't she? Isn't she?' she repeated forcefully but with a break in her voice that brought tears of mingled embarrassment and rage to her eyes. She dashed at them furiously and took up her glass.

'You sound as if you're jealous of Samantha . . .'

She whirled round, spilling some of her drink. 'Not

jealous,' she spat at him, 'just tired of being made to look a fool by my own husband to his former mistress and no doubt by *her* to everyone else in town. Look, if you want to go and sleep with her, do it. Just don't keep making fun of me! Is that a whole lot to ask?'

What am I saying? she thought distractedly, and closed her eyes in pain.

'Miranda. *Miranda!*'

Her eyes flew open. 'I'm sorry,' she whispered. 'I didn't really mean that. It's just . . .' She backed away as Nick stood up and took her arm.

'Sit down,' he said roughly. 'No, you're not going anywhere just yet,' he added as she tried to pull away. 'Because I'm going to tell you once and for all about Samantha Seymour.' He pushed her down unceremoniously into the chair and wrested the almost empty glass from her fingers. Then he scanned her white face and the way her lips trembled and turned away to pour her another drink.

'See if you can drink this one instead of spilling it,' he said as he handed her the glass.

He watched her sip the brandy, but didn't speak until some vestige of colour came back to her cheeks. Then he said quietly, 'I've only discussed you with Samantha three times, Miranda, and I happen to be able to recall exactly what I said on each occasion. The first time was when she asked me about you after that dinner party at the apartment. Whether I thought it wise to have such a young, attractive domestic—her word—working for me because mightn't people start imagining things? I replied rather flippantly, I'm afraid, possibly because I was irritated with her nosiness. I said I thought it was a very good idea, but if I were your boy-friend Bill Hartley, I probably wouldn't think it wise at all.'

'. . . Oh,' was all Miranda could find to say.

'As you say,' Nick commented with just a spark of amusement in his eyes as he watched her carefully. 'Now I don't know how she managed to twist that out of context or add to it, but I gather she did when she found you in the apartment that morning?'

'Yes,' Miranda said barely audibly.

'The third time we discussed you was several weeks ago on the day I bought your car. The paperwork wasn't quite finished on it when I went to collect it, so I went into the coffee shop next door. Samantha was there, her car was in for a service, concidentally, and,' he shrugged and looked suddenly weary again, 'because I can't spend the rest of my life avoiding her, we sat together. It came out about the car when the garage bloke came in to tell me it was ready. He knew it was for my wife and being no fan of women drivers, I presume, he pointed to it through the window and said something about red being a good colour. And I said to *him* something like . . . I guess you can see it coming, can't you? Samantha chimed in then with something about hadn't Miranda been in court over a traffic accident. And that's when I left her, and that's *exactly* how it was, Miranda,' he said evenly. 'Not quite the version she favoured you all with last night over dinner.'

Miranda stared at him. 'Then you did hear it all?'

'I didn't. Sarah rang me this morning.' He drained his glass and poured himself another drink.

'And . . . and the second time?' Miranda stammered.

Nick didn't answer immediately. Then he said deliberately, 'The only other time your name came up was when she delivered your message to me at the hospital that morning. It occurred to me what might have happened and I'm afraid I was rather brutal with her.' He shrugged and walked over to the window. It was now pouring outside.

After a minute he turned back to her and said bleakly, 'Miranda, I'm not particularly proud of the way I treated Samantha. I can't deny that I wasn't aware of Lilian's . . . expectations, and Lawrence's, I guess, but I never deliberately let her think I'd marry her. From the start—and I don't altogether agree with your description of her as my mistress, because it was a sort of on-off affair for years—but right from the start I made it clear I wasn't in the marriage stakes, and if she wanted to play along, it was her choice. She seemed perfectly content, or so I thought, when I bothered to think about it all. Which was my mistake, I admit.'

He looked down sombrely at his glass and his voice was dry when he continued. 'But then she came and told me you'd gone and she was sort of purring like a sly, contented cat and I knew I had to finish with her for ever.' He drained the glass and set it down on the coffee table with a click. He said abruptly, 'I told her it was a pity you'd gone because you were the girl I'd decided to marry, and that I'd find you if it was the last thing I did.'

Miranda felt a strange sensation at the pit of her stomach, but she forced herself to examine it critically. Hadn't just that same kind of thing betrayed her before? And what does it all mean anyway? she asked herself, and had to put her glass down because her hands had started to shake. Perhaps he's only trying to tell me he married me to get Samantha off his back . . .

'Do you understand what I'm trying to say, Miranda?' Nick asked, his voice cutting through her thoughts.

She looked up and met his dark probing gaze fleetingly. 'I don't know,' she murmured nervously. 'I . . . didn't understand about . . . Lilian or Samantha.' I'm still not sure if I understand, she thought. Why couldn't he have told me before this?

It seemed he read her thoughts, because he said with a curiously wry inflection, 'Those kind of things aren't the least awkward to explain, I'm afraid. It's not easy to discuss one woman with another, particularly when you feel . . . a little guilty as I did.'

'Oh. Well, I . . . I mean I don't . . .'

'Still don't understand?' he asked idly. 'Then I'll have to spell it out for you, won't I?' He put out a hand. 'Like I always have,' he said very quietly.

'No!' Miranda shrank back and then sprang up agitatedly and stumbled across the room. Nick made no attempt to detain her or follow her, just stood watching her. Then he said at last, almost gently, 'Does this mean you still don't want to stay married to me, Miranda?'

'. . . Yes,' she whispered, and breathed deeply.

'Why?'

'Why?' she said tightly. 'Because I fell in *love* with you, that's *why*! And it's made me so miserable I could die!' There, she thought with a gulping sob. It's out—Heaven help me!

He said with an effort, 'That seems like a good reason to stay with me if anything. Not the misery bit, but if you love me...'

'Well, it's not,' she said desperately. 'If I feel like this now how miserable will I feel when you start to get tired of me? And it's not, because all these explanations don't—I mean, I appreciate them, but they don't change the fact that I'm still the girl . . . you said that day in court I wasn't really your type. Do you think I don't know why you've kept out of sight of everybody?' she asked painfully, and bit her lip at the flash of anger in his eyes.

She looked down at her hands then and breathed deeply. 'I'm sorry,' she said huskily at last. 'This must be very embarrassing for you. I didn't want it to happen, but I just couldn't help it. So you see it's better I go now—truly.'

'*Look* at me, Miranda,' Nick commanded quietly.

She did eventually, with a hot flood of colour to her cheeks. His eyes were darker than ever, she thought inconsequently, and for once not mocking or amused or contemptuous. He feels sorry for me now, she thought.

But his next words surprised her.

'When did you fall in love with me, Miranda?'

'I . . . I'm not sure,' she stammered, taken aback. 'Does it matter?'

'I suppose not,' he murmured with a shadow of a smile in his eyes. 'I just wondered if it was the same time . . . or rather one of the times I fell in love with you. It kept happening, you see,' he said gravely. 'Only, in my cynicism, I kept refusing to accept it,' he added with self-directed irony.

Miranda's mouth dropped open and he smiled, not pleasantly, as if that same irony was biting deep into him.

'My dear,' he said unevenly, 'didn't you think it strange, any of these things I've told you tonight? Aren't they really the right explanations? Since I've got to know you I've committed just about every act of lunacy a sane rational man can—unless he happens to be deeply in love. I bearded Bill Hartley in his den in a manner of speaking, I used my own sister as a bait to dangle in front of you, I *married* you when I could have just slept with you. And I didn't just sleep with you, Miranda, ever. Because that would never have been enough for me. I needed you to respond to me, like I responded to you. I needed you to want it as much as I did, to want *me* and only me. Didn't you know that?'

Miranda sat down unexpectedly on the settee as her knees gave way.

'I didn't know much about that part of it,' she said faintly. 'I didn't know what to expect.'

'But you did know enough about men to say to me once that a sensitive, intelligent lover was more important than . . . other things. Did I qualify?' he asked, with his eyes searching her face.

'Oh yes,' she whispered, and coloured deliciously beneath his scrutiny. 'But you never *said* anything,' she added helplessly.

'Neither did you, for that matter, my beautiful, naïve bride,' he answered gravely.

'Well, I had a reason—I think,' she said dazedly.

Nick smiled slightly. 'It seems we both had. Can I tell you mine?'

She nodded wordlessly.

He didn't speak immediately and when he did it was on a strangely harsh note. 'I didn't believe it could ever happen to me. I think I told you I didn't believe in love. So when I finally admitted it had happened to me, that the state did exist, I had to keep testing it, probing it, looking for flaws. Then too,' he went on flatly, 'I saw what it had done to Sarah, and for the first time I understood, and it made me very wary. And sometimes unbelievably cruel.'

Miranda stared at him wide-eyed and then held her breath as he came to sit down beside her.

'But then again, at other times,' he said with such a look of flashing amusement that she trembled, 'living with you—well, it wasn't making me miserable, that much I do know, but the opposite. I couldn't believe it at first, such domestic bliss. Only,' he sobered, 'I was haunted by something I said to you the first time I asked you to sleep with me.'

She moved suddenly, then quietened like a bird in a storm.

'Something about helping you along the road so that you could anywhere become anything,' he went on his voice strangely bleak. 'I tried to persuade myself that I was keeping you out of sight to protect you from Lilian and Samantha. But it was much more. I wanted to build a high wall around us with tall gates and throw away the key. Except perhaps to Sarah, because she really needed you too. And the real reason was a lot simpler. You never needed my help, Miranda. It's all there within you and always was. And I knew I wasn't the first, wouldn't be the last man to know that. What I didn't know and what tormented the life out of me was the thought that *I* might not be your heart's desire.'

'I didn't know,' she said slowly, not quite believing what she was hearing.

'Didn't you?' he said sombrely. 'Didn't you ever stop to wonder why I taunted you with your country origins, your clothes—every weapon I could think of, not because *I* believed it, but because I wanted *you* to believe it so that you wouldn't have the confidence to leave me. My darling, you could take your place anywhere,' he said, his voice slightly unsteady. 'You have inborn in you far greater qualities than you could have ever learnt from me.'

They stared at each other until he said, 'Men are supposed to be so rational, aren't they? I thought I was. It took the thought of you, the girl I took to bed here for the first time, so true, so beautiful——' he hesitated and then went on with an effort, 'it took the thought of . . . you with someone else to make me understand. That was one of the times I fell in love with you, by the way,' he added softly.

He reached out and touched her hair as he spoke

and there was nothing weary or cynical in his eyes as they slid over her.

'You were so angry with me last night,' Miranda whispered involuntarily.

'Yes.' He didn't deny it. 'When I arrived in time to hear you say you'd married the wrong man, I could have strangled you on the spot. Didn't that give you a clue?' he asked idly, but his eyes were curiously watchful.

'You believed it?' she said shakily.

'Nick slid the ribbon off her hair and spread his fingers through it before answering. Then he said abruptly, 'I was jealous of the thought of you and any man. But one man, particularly. I know I can be insufferable on occasions, Miranda, and I have to admit I went up to see Bill Hartley thinking it was only some hillbilly I had to wrest you from. But I came away liking him and respecting him—and very conscious that I was up against a formidable opponent, someone who'd had the strength to let you go.'

His fingers massaging her scalp became more urgent as he went on, looking oddly grim, 'Last night, when I heard you say what you did, I knew—or rather I thought I knew, how very wise he'd been.'

It was pouring now, great gusts of rain flinging angrily at the windows, but Miranda was unconscious of the storm. She was still trying to grasp the unbelievable.

'Did Bill know why you wanted to find me?'

'I think he might have guessed,' he said solemnly. 'I arrived up there at five o'clock in the morning feeling slightly ... demented. Then too, he said a strange thing as we parted. He said, don't underestimate Miranda, and don't hurt her, because you'd have me to reckon with then.'

She didn't attempt to stem the tears that flowed down her cheeks. 'I did love him in a way,' she whispered. 'But I think he always knew it wasn't the way he would have wanted it to be.'

She looked at Nick and saw him close his eyes briefly. Then his hand slid down to close around her shoulders and pull her into his arms.

'Miranda,' he said hoarsely, his lips just touching the corner of her mouth, 'my darling, if you knew how long I've waited for you to say that!'

It was a long lingering kiss, almost as if they were kissing for the first time, and when she finally lay flushed and dishevelled in his lap, her heart was beating wildly, because he had never been so exquisitely tender with her before yet at the same time arousing her so completely.

His fingers trembled as they rested on the buttons of her blouse, then he breathed deeply as his dark gaze roamed from her swelling breasts to her lips, to her eyes.

'This is when I should be asking you to marry me, Miranda,' he said with an effort, his voice deep and unsteady. 'But,' his eyes glinted suddenly with just a shadow of his former amusement, 'seeing we jumped the gun a little there, I think we could proceed to the next stage, don't you?'

Miranda stared up at him with her lips parted and, in her eyes, the last tiny shred of uncertainty.

The amusement fled and with a groan Nick gathered her closer and murmured into her hair, 'I think we should set about making a baby . . .'

'Oh Nick,' she whispered joyously when she could speak at last. 'Yes, please!'

AUSTRALIA'S NATIONAL DESSERT

When the famous Russian ballerina Anna Pavlova visited Australia in the early part of this century, the chef at her Sydney hotel served her a new dessert, which he named after her and which has since become an Australian national dish.

To make pavlova you need:

  waxed paper
  4 egg whites, room temperature
  ¼ tsp. salt
  ¼ tsp. cream of tartar
  1 cup fine white sugar
  2 cups sweetened whipped cream
  3 cups fruit of your choice

Preheat oven to 250°F. (130°C.). Line a cookie sheet with waxed paper and grease lightly, then draw an 8-inch-diameter circle in middle of sheet. In a bowl beat egg whites until foamy, then add salt and cream of tartar. Continue to beat until stiff glossy peaks form. Add sugar gradually and beat for 2 minutes. Place half of meringue in circle, then spread and flatten to circle's edges with back of a metal spoon. With a pastry tube, pipe remaining meringue around edge of circle, building sides to a height of 4 inches and leaving a large hollow in center. Place in oven and bake for 1½ hours; take care not to let the "shell" become too brown. Turn off oven, open door and allow shell to sit for five minutes. Remove from oven, transfer to a cooling tray and let stand until thoroughly cooled. Remove waxed paper, transfer to a serving plate and fill with whipped cream and fruit.

HARLEQUIN
PREMIERE AUTHOR EDITIONS

6 top Harlequin authors—6 of their best books!

1. JANET DAILEY Giant of Mesabi
2. CHARLOTTE LAMB Dark Master
3. ROBERTA LEIGH Heart of the Lion
4. ANNE MATHER Legacy of the Past
5. ANNE WEALE Stowaway
6. VIOLET WINSPEAR The Burning Sands

Harlequin is proud to offer these 6 exciting romance novels by 6 of our most popular authors. In brand-new beautifully designed covers, each Harlequin Premiere Author Edition is a bestselling love story—a contemporary, compelling and passionate read to remember!

Available in September wherever paperback books are sold, *or* through Harlequin Reader Service. Simply complete and mail the coupon below.
